ETERNAL SURRENDER

Laura Shenton

ETERNAL SURRENDER

Laura Shenton

Iridescent Toad Publishing

Iridescent Toad Publishing.

First edition. ISBN 978-1-913779-58-0

Chapter One

The coach rattled over the cobblestones of Ruehaven's northern quarter, its polished black exterior reflecting the dim glow of gas lamps that lined the streets like sentinels against the encroaching dusk. The wheels clattered rhythmically, a sound that had become as familiar to Ritchie Caldwell as his own footsteps over the countless journeys of his extraordinarily long life. Inside the velvet-lined interior, he adjusted his cravat, pale fingers moving with methodical precision. The silk felt cool against his skin – one of the few tactile pleasures that hadn't diminished with the passing years. Such were the mundane adaptations of immortality, these small rituals that anchored him to a semblance of humanity.

The faint scent of leather and polish permeated the coach's interior, mingling with the subtle aroma of the pomade that kept Ritchie's dark hair immaculately styled. He gazed out the window at the passing streets, watching the townspeople hurry about their mortal business, their brief lives burning so brightly compared to his endless existence.

"Almost there, my Lord," called the driver from above, his voice cutting through the steady drumming of hooves and the creaking of well-oiled springs.

Ritchie nodded despite knowing the gesture would go unseen, a private acknowledgment of the message received. Several hundred years of existence had taught him that maintaining certain human courtesies helped preserve what remained of his humanity – a precious commodity he'd guarded with increasing vigilance as the decades blurred together. The carriage slowed as they approached Whitfield's Stables, an establishment known throughout the county for breeding the finest horses in the region. The distinct aroma of hay, horse, and well-tanned leather wafted through the air, growing stronger as they drew nearer.

As the carriage came to a halt with a gentle lurch, Ritchie straightened his already impeccable jacket and adjusted the silver-headed cane at his side. He stepped out with fluid grace, his tall figure cutting an imposing silhouette. The air hung heavy with the promise of rain, the clouds overhead swollen and dark against the fading daylight. Despite the threatening weather, he had chosen to venture out rather than postpone his errand. His current team of horses were ageing beyond their prime, their once-powerful strides now showing the inevitable decline that afflicted all mortal creatures. He preferred to select replacements personally rather than delegate such matters to his staff, no matter how loyal or competent they might be.

"Wait here, Gregory," he instructed his driver, his voice carrying the subtle weight of authority that came naturally after years of command. "This shouldn't take long."

Gregory, a weathered man of fifty with a face lined by years of service and outdoor work, tipped his hat in acknowledgment. He had served Ritchie for nearly fifteen years without ever questioning his master's peculiar habits

– the nocturnal schedule, the carefully drawn curtains during daylight hours, the specific dietary requirements. Loyalty and discretion were well compensated in Ritchie's household, and Gregory had proven himself exceptional in both regards.

The stable yard was a hive of activity, with grooms leading horses to and from the paddocks and stable hands carrying buckets and bales of hay. As Ritchie's presence registered among the workers, a hush fell over the yard, followed by hurried whispers. The stable owner, Harold Whitfield, a stout man with ruddy cheeks and a perpetual sheen of sweat on his brow, hurried over when he spotted Ritchie. His breathing was laboured from the exertion, small beads of perspiration gathering at his temples despite the cool air.

Few in Ruehaven didn't recognise the reclusive lord of the northern castle, with his aristocratic features and the subtle aura of danger that seemed to emanate from him like a cold draft. Fewer still didn't know the rumours that surrounded him – tales of unnatural longevity, of servants who disappeared without trace, of strange sounds echoing from the castle on moonless nights. Rumours that, while exaggerated by superstitious minds and embellished with each retelling, weren't entirely unfounded.

"Lord Caldwell! What an unexpected honour," Whitfield gushed, bowing slightly, his hands nervously straightening his waistcoat. "Had I known you were coming, I would have prepared a proper welcome. Perhaps refreshments, or…"

Ritchie waved away the formality with a graceful motion of his hand, a single gold signet ring catching what little light filtered through the clouds. "I prefer unannounced visits, Mr Whitfield. They tend to reveal the true nature of an establishment." His eyes, dark and penetrating, surveyed the yard with the assessment of one who missed no detail, however insignificant it might seem to others.

"Of course, of course," Whitfield agreed hastily, a forced smile stretching across his fleshy face. "Very wise, my Lord. Very wise indeed. You're interested in horses, I presume? We have several magnificent stallions that would suit your coach. Strong, obedient creatures, the lot of them. Bred from the finest bloodlines in the country, I assure you."

"I'd like to see them," Ritchie replied, his voice carrying the slight accent of a time long past, barely perceptible to modern ears but hinting at origins far removed from the present day. Each syllable was precisely enunciated, a relic of an era when speech was an art form rather than merely a means of communication.

Whitfield nodded eagerly, gesturing towards the main stable building with its freshly painted doors and clean-swept entrance. "Right this way, my Lord. I think you'll be most impressed with what we have to offer. I'll show you our best specimens, knowing your discerning taste from your previous purchases."

As Whitfield led him across the yard, Ritchie's senses – far more acute than those of the mortals surrounding him – picked up countless details: the varying heartbeats of the stable hands who watched him with wary eyes, the nervous shuffling of horses in their stalls sensing a predator in their midst, the multitude of scents that told stories the humans around him would never perceive. He had long since learnt to filter this overwhelming sensory information, focusing only on what might prove useful or interesting.

They had nearly reached the main stable entrance when a commotion erupted from a side building – angry shouts, the sound of something heavy falling, followed by jeering laughter and what might have been a cry of pain, quickly stifled.

Ritchie's head turned sharply towards the disturbance, his preternatural hearing pinpointing its exact location. "What's that?" he enquired, though it was less a question than a demand for explanation.

Whitfield's face flushed a deeper red, his pulse quickening in a way that Ritchie could both hear and sense. "Nothing of concern, my Lord. Just the stable boys roughhousing, as young men do. I'll have them disciplined later for the disturbance. Most unprofessional, especially with you visiting. Please, let me show you the stallions I mentioned..."

But Ritchie was already moving towards the noise, drawn by something he couldn't quite identify. It wasn't hunger – he had fed well before venturing out, as he always did when business would bring him into close proximity with humans. No, it was something else entirely. The smell of fear, perhaps, or the particular quality of anguish in one of the voices – a timbre that resonated with something deep within him, striking a chord of recognition that he hadn't felt in decades.

His boots crunched purposefully on the gravel as he strode towards the side building, Whitfield hurrying behind him with stammered protests that fell on deaf ears. The structure was smaller than the main stables, likely used for storage or as quarters for some of the workers. The wooden door was weathered, its paint peeling at the edges from years of exposure to the elements.

He pushed it open without hesitation, the hinges groaning in protest at the sudden movement. The scene inside revealed itself in stark clarity to his enhanced vision, despite the dimness of the interior. Five men, ranging in age from their early twenties to middle age, were crowded in a loose circle, their laughter dying abruptly as the door swung open. At the centre of their attention, sprawled in the hay that covered the packed earth floor, was a young man with tousled blond hair that caught what little light filtered through the dusty windows.

The fallen young man's shirt was torn at the shoulder, revealing pale skin already darkening with bruises that would bloom into vivid purple by morning. A thin trickle of blood ran from the corner of his mouth, its metallic scent immediately registering in Ritchie's consciousness. Despite being sprawled on his back and obviously mistreated, there was a defiance in the young man's blue eyes that struck Ritchie like a jolt – a spark of something that refused to be extinguished, a silent declaration that while his body might be momentarily defeated, his spirit remained unbroken.

"What is the meaning of this?" Ritchie's voice cut through the sudden silence like a blade of ice, though perhaps that was merely the effect of his cold fury becoming palpable in the confined space.

The men froze, turning to face the intruder one by one. Recognition dawned on their faces in succession, followed swiftly by fear – the instinctive, primal dread that prey feels in the presence of a predator. They shifted uneasily, exchanging glances and silently determining who would speak first.

"L-Lord Caldwell," one of them finally stammered, a burly man with a beard that did little to hide the nervous working of his jaw. "We were just... he was..."

"He was stealing, my Lord," another supplied quickly, finding his courage. "Caught him trying to pocket some of the tack money. We were just teaching him a lesson about honesty, as is proper."

The young man on the ground pushed himself up to his elbows, wincing at the movement. A strand of blond hair fell across his forehead, and he brushed it aside with a gesture that held surprising dignity given his circumstances. "I wasn't stealing anything," he countered, his voice steady despite the slight rasp of pain. "I was counting my earnings, which apparently is a crime if you don't do it where they can all watch and make sure you don't get a penny more than they think you deserve."

There was something in the young man's voice – a refined quality, an educated cadence that seemed at odds with his current employment and state. His diction and the structure of his response suggested a background and education far beyond what one would expect from a stable hand. Ritchie found himself intrigued despite his better judgment, captivated by the incongruity of this elegant mind trapped in such coarse circumstances.

"Leave us," Ritchie commanded, his tone leaving no room for argument or discussion.

The men shuffled out, their earlier bravado entirely evaporated in the face of Ritchie's authority. Whitfield herded them with apologetic glances towards Ritchie, murmuring assurances that they would be dealt with appropriately. When the door closed behind them with a dull thud, Ritchie approached the young man, extending a hand in a gesture that surprised even himself with its spontaneity.

"Can you stand?" he asked, his voice modulated to a gentler tone than he had used with the others.

The blond looked at the offered hand with suspicion, his blue eyes narrowing as he assessed Ritchie's intentions. After a moment of hesitation, he tentatively reached out to accept the assistance. As their skin touched, Ritchie felt an unexpected surge – not of hunger, as he might have anticipated given his nature, but of something else entirely. A connection, immediate and undeniable, like a key turning in a lock that had long been sealed shut.

"Thank you," the young man said as he gained his feet, brushing hay from his clothes with as much dignity as one could muster in such circumstances. His movements, though pained, carried a natural grace. "Though I don't know why you bothered. Most gentlemen wouldn't interrupt their business to concern themselves with a stable hand's troubles."

"I am not most gentlemen," Ritchie replied, studying the young man's features with undisguised interest. "And neither, I suspect, are you a typical stable hand."

Ritchie paused, surprising himself with his honesty. In centuries of existence, he had learnt the value of careful words and measured responses. Yet something about this encounter had stripped away those layers of caution, leaving an uncharacteristic candour in their place.

"What's your name?" he asked firmly.

"Tobias. Tobias Marlow." The young man straightened to his full height, which still left him several inches shorter than Ritchie's imposing stature. There was pride in his bearing despite the dirt that smudged his face and the blood that was beginning to dry at the corner of his mouth.

"How long have you worked here, Tobias Marlow?" Ritchie asked, finding himself genuinely curious about the circumstances that had brought someone of obvious refinement to such a lowly position.

Tobias straightened his torn shirt self-consciously, his fingers deft despite what must have been painful bruising on his ribs and back. His hands, though now calloused from manual labour, showed the long fingers and well-shaped nails of someone raised to handle books and pens rather than pitchforks and saddles. "Six months. Not by choice, I assure you. My family's fortunes took a rather dramatic turn, and I found myself in need of employment. Beggars, as they say, cannot be choosers."

"And is this how you're regularly treated?" Ritchie gestured to the bruises beginning to form on Tobias' visible skin, his voice carrying a dangerous edge that would have made some men tremble.

Tobias' mouth quirked in a bitter smile that transformed his face, lending it a charm that was all the more compelling for its lack of artifice. "Only on days ending in 'y', my Lord," he replied, a flash of wit revealing itself beneath the layers of caution.

Ritchie found himself smiling in response, an unusual occurrence that felt almost foreign on his features. It had been decades since anyone had amused him so genuinely, since he had felt such an immediate connection to another being. "Would you consider alternative employment?" he asked, the words emerging before he had fully considered their implications.

"What sort of alternative?" Suspicion rose in

Tobias' eyes, the wariness of one who had learnt through hard experience that unexpected offers often came with hidden costs.

"I find myself in need of a personal assistant," Ritchie elaborated, warming to the idea as he spoke it aloud. "Someone literate, observant, and discreet. The pay would be considerably better than whatever pittance Whitfield offers, and I can guarantee no one at my estate would dare lay a hand on you." This last was stated with absolute certainty – a simple fact rather than a mere promise.

Tobias studied him, his gaze far more penetrating than most mortals would dare direct at Ritchie. The young man's heartbeat had accelerated slightly, a mixture of hope and trepidation evident in its rhythm. "Why would you offer such a position to a complete stranger? For all you know, I could be exactly what they accused me of – a thief looking for an opportunity."

"Call it instinct," Ritchie replied, holding that searching gaze without discomfort. "I've lived long enough to trust my judgment of character." The slight emphasis on 'long' was unconscious, a rare slip that hinted at his true nature.

Something in his wording made Tobias' eyes narrow slightly, a flash of perception that suggested the young man had caught the unintentional implication. But whatever suspicions might have been awakened were apparently outweighed by the practical considerations of his current circumstances.

"When would you want me to start?" Tobias asked after a moment of consideration, his tone carefully neutral despite the opportunity being presented.

"Immediately. Gather whatever belongings you wish to bring. My coach is outside." Ritchie gestured towards the door, already considering the logistics of integrating this unexpected addition into his household.

As Tobias nodded and moved to collect his few possessions from a corner of the stable, Ritchie watched him, puzzled by his own impulsive decision. In centuries of existence, he had rarely acted on such immediate impulse, preferring careful deliberation to spontaneous action. Yet something about

Tobias Marlow called to him – awakened feelings he had thought long dormant beneath the weight of endless years.

Protection, yes. The desire to shield this bright, defiant spirit from further harm at the hands of lesser men. But also possession. The unmistakable urge to claim Tobias as his own, to keep him close, to discover every facet of his mind and personality. And beneath those impulses, simmering like banked embers, was desire – a hunger different from but no less potent than his need for blood.

It had been decades since Ritchie had allowed himself such indulgences, having learnt through painful experience the complications that arose from becoming too attached to ephemeral mortals. The intensity of his reaction to this young man was both unexpected and unsettling, challenging the careful control he had maintained for longer than Tobias had been alive.

But as Tobias returned, a small bundle clutched in his hands and a determined set to his jaw, Ritchie knew he had made his decision. For better or worse, their fates were now intertwined, drawn together by forces Ritchie himself didn't fully understand but was powerless to resist.

"Ready, my Lord," Tobias said, his voice steady despite the uncertainty that must have been churning within him. The decision to leave with a virtual stranger – especially one surrounded by the whispered rumours that clung to Ritchie like shadows – spoke volumes about the desperate nature of his current circumstances.

"Then let us depart," Ritchie replied, holding the door open with a courtly gesture that belonged to another era. "I believe, Mr Marlow, that this may be the beginning of a most interesting arrangement."

As they walked back to the waiting coach, Ritchie felt something stir within his chest – a sensation so foreign that it took him a moment to recognise it as intense anticipation. The endless years had long since dulled his expectations of novelty or surprise; very little astonished him anymore. The world repeated its patterns with only minor variations – never enough to disguise their essential sameness.

But something told him that Tobias Marlow would prove to be the exception to that rule. A bright flame in the gathering darkness of eternity. A challenge to his carefully constructed isolation. Perhaps even a danger to the barriers he had built around what remained of his heart.

And for once, Ritchie found himself looking forward to being proven right.

Chapter Two

The imposing silhouette of Caldwell Castle appeared on the horizon just as night began to settle over Ruehaven. Tobias leaned forward slightly in his seat, unable to mask his awe as the gothic spires emerged from the deepening shadows, their jagged points piercing the indigo sky like ancient weapons. He had seen the castle from a distance many times, of course – everyone in Ruehaven had – but he'd never imagined he would one day approach it.

Yet here he sat, in Lord Caldwell's private coach, the plush velvet seats unfamiliar against his rough-worn clothes. He had been plucked from squalor and abuse on what seemed little more than a whim, rescued by a nobleman whose reputation in town was as mysterious as it was foreboding. The situation was so improbable that Tobias half expected to wake up back in the stable's hayloft, the entire encounter nothing more than a desperate dream conjured by his battered body seeking escape from reality.

"Impressive, isn't it?" Ritchie's voice interrupted his thoughts, the rich baritone filling the confined space of the coach. "Though I suppose after a time, one becomes accustomed to anything."

Tobias turned to find his new employer watching him with a curious intensity that sent an involuntary shiver up his spine – not entirely unpleasant, but unsettling nonetheless. The nobleman's eyes seemed to absorb the limited light rather than reflect it, pools of darkness that hinted at unfathomable depths.

"I doubt I could ever become accustomed to such grandeur," Tobias admitted, his voice barely above a whisper, as though speaking too loudly might shatter the moment. "It seems... otherworldly."

A slight smile played at the corner of Ritchie's mouth, revealing nothing, yet suggesting volumes. "An apt description, though perhaps not in the way you intend."

Before Tobias could ask what he meant, the coach passed through the massive iron gates with a resonant creak that echoed like a warning bell. They began the winding ascent to the castle, the wheels crunching against the gravelled path. Ancient oak trees lined the way, their gnarled branches reaching towards each other like supplicants, creating a canopy that deepened the shadows. The air grew noticeably cooler as they progressed, carrying with it the scent of damp earth and something else – something older and less definable that made Tobias' nostrils flare with unconscious recognition.

When they finally reached the courtyard, the coach came to a halt before a broad set of steps leading to massive oak doors carved with scenes Tobias couldn't quite discern in the darkness. A small retinue of servants emerged from various entrances, moving with the quiet efficiency of those long accustomed to their duties. Their faces were impassive, betraying neither curiosity nor judgment as they assessed the coach's unexpected passenger.

Ritchie descended first, his movements fluid and graceful despite his tall frame. He turned to offer Tobias his hand, the pale skin nearly luminous in the gloom. The gesture was oddly chivalrous, something Tobias might have expected towards a lady of quality rather than a former stable hand with dirt still embedded beneath his fingernails. Nevertheless, he accepted, acutely aware of the coolness of Ritchie's skin against his own, the nobleman's fingers surprisingly strong as they clasped his own.

"Welcome to Caldwell Castle, Mr Marlow," Ritchie said as Tobias' feet touched the cobblestones. "Your new home, should you wish it to be."

The words hung in the air between them, weighted with unspoken meanings that Tobias couldn't yet decipher but instinctively felt. Home. The concept seemed foreign after his fortunes had declined.

An elderly man with impeccable posture and a face lined with the wisdom of decades stepped forward, bowing slightly. His black suit was pristine, his white hair perfectly groomed. "My Lord, we weren't expecting your return until much later. Shall I have dinner prepared?"

"Yes, thank you, Hawthorne. And please have a room prepared for Mr Marlow in the east wing. He will be joining my household as my personal assistant."

If Hawthorne was surprised by this announcement, he showed no sign of it, his expression remaining as impassive as carved marble. Tobias wondered fleetingly if all the castle's servants were trained in such perfect emotional restraint. "Very good, my Lord. Will Mr Marlow be dining with you this evening?"

Ritchie glanced at Tobias, taking in his dishevelled appearance with a sweeping gaze that missed nothing – the smudges of dirt that still clung to his face, the torn seam at his shoulder, the way he unconsciously tried to stand straighter under scrutiny. There was no disgust in the assessment, only practical consideration.

"Perhaps not immediately. I believe Mr Marlow would appreciate an opportunity to refresh himself first. Have a bath drawn and find him suitable attire. We'll dine in two hours."

"As you wish, my Lord," Hawthorne replied, his voice carrying the faintest hint of an accent Tobias couldn't place. The butler then turned to Tobias, his eyes revealing nothing of his thoughts about his master's new acquisition. "If you'll follow me, sir."

Tobias hesitated, looking to Ritchie, suddenly reluctant to be separated from the one familiar element in this unfamiliar world, despite their short acquaintance. The realisation of his own dependency disturbed him – had his circumstances so reduced him that he now clung to any show of kindness like a drowning man to driftwood?

"Go," Ritchie encouraged with a small nod, seeming to understand Tobias' unspoken concern. "Hawthorne will see to your needs. I have matters to attend to before dinner, but I look forward to our conversation later."

There was something in Ritchie's tone – a subtle undercurrent of anticipation – that made Tobias' pulse quicken. The words were innocuous, yet delivered with a certain emphasis that suggested layers of meaning beneath the surface. With a nod of his own, Tobias followed Hawthorne into the castle, conscious of Ritchie's gaze following him until the heavy doors closed behind them with a resonant thud that seemed to mark the final severance from his old life.

The interior was even more impressive than the façade, with soaring ceilings that disappeared into shadow, intricate tapestries depicting scenes from mythology and history, and furnishings that spoke of wealth accumulated over generations. Crystal chandeliers hung like frozen waterfalls, their candles casting dancing shadows across marble floors and wood-panelled walls. Portraits of stern-faced men and women watched from gilded frames, their eyes seeming to track Tobias' progress through their domain.

Yet despite the grandeur, the castle possessed a peculiar stillness, as though time moved differently within its walls. The usual sounds of a large household – the bustling of servants, the clatter from kitchens, the general hum of human activity – were eerily absent, replaced by a profound silence broken only by their footsteps and the occasional distant closing of a door.

Hawthorne led him through a maze of

corridors, each seemingly identical to the last, up a sweeping staircase of polished oak that didn't creak despite its apparent age, and finally to a door of dark, polished wood adorned with intricate carvings of vines and flowers. "Your chambers, Mr Marlow. I trust you'll find everything to your satisfaction."

The butler opened the door with a small brass key, which he then presented to Tobias with a slight bow. "This is yours. Lord Caldwell insists that all residents have complete privacy within their own quarters."

Tobias accepted the key, its weight in his palm unexpectedly significant. Privacy and security – two luxuries that had seemed elusively impossible before. He stepped into a room larger than the entire house his family had inhabited before their fall from grace. A four-poster bed dominated one wall, draped in rich burgundy velvet that matched the heavy curtains framing tall windows. A fireplace took up another wall, flames already dancing merrily within its marble surround, casting a warm glow that softened the room's grandeur. Plush rugs covered portions of the hardwood floor, their intricate patterns hinting at distant origins. A writing desk stood beneath one window, equipped with quills, ink, and pristine paper. A door to the side presumably led to a dressing room or washroom.

"This is... all for me?" Tobias couldn't keep the astonishment from his voice, his eyes wide as he tried to absorb the luxury surrounding him.

"Indeed, sir. Lord Caldwell is a generous employer to those who serve him well." There was something in Hawthorne's tone that suggested additional meaning, a certain knowing quality that piqued Tobias' curiosity. But before he could enquire, the elderly servant continued, "A bath is being prepared as we speak. I shall take the liberty of selecting some garments that should fit you adequately until proper measurements can be taken. Will there be anything else you require?"

Still overwhelmed by the sudden transformation of his circumstances, Tobias shook his head, his fingers unconsciously stroking the soft fabric of a nearby chair. "No, thank you. This is more than sufficient."

Hawthorne nodded once, his expression

softening almost imperceptibly. "Dinner will be served in the main dining room. I shall return to escort you at the appropriate time."

After Hawthorne departed, closing the door with a soft click, Tobias stood motionless for several moments, simply absorbing the sudden silence and solitude. Then, as though breaking free from a trance, he began to explore his new quarters with growing wonderment. The bed was draped in linens of exquisite material, finer than anything he'd known even before his family's downfall – sheets of soft, cool linen, a thick duvet that seemed to shimmer in the light, and a velvet throw at the foot, so plush it seemed to swallow his fingers as he stroked it. He ran his hands over the fabric, marvelling at textures so inviting to his calloused touch.

The washroom revealed an enormous copper tub being filled by two maids who curtsied and departed as soon as they noticed his presence, leaving behind the lingering scent of lavender and rosemary rising with the steam. Towels fluffy enough to sleep on were stacked nearby, alongside crystal bottles containing what appeared to be oils and soaps.

As he sank into the hot water sometime later, a groan of pleasure escaping his lips, Tobias found himself questioning the extraordinary turn his life had taken. The heat penetrated muscles long accustomed to strain and abuse, dissolving knots of tension he hadn't even realised he carried. Dirt and grime from the stables swirled away in the water, as though washing away his former existence along with the physical evidence of it.

Why had Lord Caldwell chosen him? What exactly would be expected of him as a personal assistant? The position seemed vague, the offer too generous for the simple duties the title suggested. There had to be more to it – no one offered such luxury without expecting something significant in return.

And then there was Lord Caldwell himself – his penetrating gaze that seemed to see through pretence, his otherworldly presence that commanded attention without effort, and the strange coldness of his touch that had lingered on Tobias' skin like a memory refusing to fade. The rumours that circulated in Ruehaven about the castle's reclusive master suddenly seemed less like idle gossip and more like warnings.

They said he never appeared during daylight hours. They whispered that servants who displeased him disappeared without trace. They spoke of strange sounds emanating from the castle on moonless nights, and of townspeople who ventured too close after dark and returned changed – if they returned at all.

Yet despite the uncertainty, despite the warnings his rational mind screamed at him, Tobias felt an undeniable pull towards Ritchie. There had been something in those dark eyes that spoke to a part of Tobias he'd long tried to ignore – a part that found a peculiar thrill in submission, in being seen and commanded by someone stronger. It was a recognition that transcended their brief acquaintance, as though Ritchie had glimpsed his soul and named something essential within it.

It was this hidden aspect of himself that had made his time at the stables so complex. The humiliation and rough treatment had been genuine hardships, painful reminders of how far he had fallen from respectability. Yet there were moments when the degradation had stirred something in him – a shameful excitement he couldn't acknowledge even to himself. Being forced to his knees, being handled roughly, being reminded of his powerlessness – these experiences had sometimes produced a confusing arousal that left him disgusted with himself afterwards.

The water cooled as Tobias' thoughts wandered these dangerous paths. Finally, he rose from the bath, his skin flushed from heat and the direction of his contemplations. He dried himself with the soft towels, then moved to the bedroom to dress in the clothes provided – a crisp white shirt with pearl buttons, dark trousers of a fit that suggested they had been waiting for him, and a waistcoat of deep burgundy.

Looking at himself in the full-length mirror that stood in one corner, he barely recognised the reflection staring back at him – clean, well-dressed, a gentleman once more, at least in appearance. The transformation was startling. With his features no longer obscured by dirt and his lean frame properly clothed, he looked like the person he might have become had fate been kinder. Only his hands, still rough from labour, and a certain wariness in his eyes betrayed his recent past.

A soft knock at the door announced Hawthorne's return, pulling Tobias from his self-assessment.

"Lord Caldwell awaits you in the dining room, Mr Marlow," the butler announced, his eyes taking in Tobias' transformation with what might have been approval.

Chapter Three

Tobias followed Hawthorne, his nervousness growing with each step. They descended to the main floor and proceeded down a corridor lined with portraits – generations of Caldwells, Tobias presumed, men and women in the attire of various eras, all bearing similar aristocratic features and haughty expressions.

Finally, they reached a set of double doors of dark, polished wood inlaid with mother-of-pearl in an intricate pattern that caught the light from nearby sconces. Hawthorne opened them with familiar ease, revealing the space beyond.

The dining room was vast, with a ceiling that rose at least twenty feet and was adorned with a fresco depicting classical scenes. It was lit by dozens of candles in silver candelabras and a crystal chandelier that cast prismatic reflections across the polished table and gleaming place settings. Heavy velvet drapes in deep blue were drawn across tall windows, and a fire crackled in a fireplace large enough for a man to stand in.

At the far end of a long mahogany table that could have seated thirty sat Ritchie, who rose as Tobias entered. His dark hair was now tied back with a ribbon, accentuating the sharp angles of his face and the unusual pallor of his complexion. He had changed as well, now wearing a tailored suit of such deep black that it seemed to absorb the candlelight rather than reflect it. The effect was both elegant and slightly unnerving, as though he existed at a slight remove from the physical world around him.

"Mr Marlow," Ritchie greeted, his voice carrying easily across the expanse between them. "You look remarkably improved."

The words were simple but delivered with an appreciation that warmed Tobias unexpectedly. He approached the table, his footsteps soundless on the thick carpet that covered the centre of the room.

"Thank you, my Lord," Tobias replied,

conscious of the vast difference in their stations despite the nobleman's apparent disregard for it. "And thank you for your generosity. The accommodations are far more luxurious than I could have anticipated."

Ritchie gestured to the chair at his right hand, rather than having Tobias sit at the opposite end of the table as protocol might have dictated. "Please, join me. And you may call me Ritchie when we're alone. 'My Lord' becomes tiresome after a time."

The invitation to such familiarity was unexpected, another breach of the social boundaries Tobias had been raised to respect. He slid into the indicated chair, noting the fine china, crystal, and silver that awaited him. "As you wish... Ritchie."

The name felt strangely intimate on his tongue, a privilege he had not earned but was being offered nonetheless. It created an immediate shift in the atmosphere between them, a subtle relaxation of formality that both relieved and disconcerted him.

Hawthorne appeared with wine, filling Tobias' glass with a ruby liquid that caught the candlelight like liquid fire. Curiously, he left Ritchie's glass untouched, which Tobias found strange but didn't remark upon. Perhaps his host preferred to pour his own drink, or had particular preferences about when to imbibe.

As the first course was served – a soup of delicate flavours Tobias didn't recognise but found delicious – Ritchie observed him with that same intense scrutiny he'd shown in the coach. His gaze was evaluative but not cold, as though he were piecing together a puzzle whose solution fascinated him.

"Tell me, Tobias," Ritchie said finally, breaking the silence that had settled between them, "what circumstances led a young man of obvious education to working in Whitfield's stables?"

The question was direct but not unkind. Tobias hesitated, absently tracing the rim of his wine glass with one finger, then decided there was little point in concealment. His story was hardly unique in these uncertain times, and Ritchie had already seen him at his lowest.

"My father made some unfortunate investments," he began, his voice steady despite the painful memories. "He trusted the wrong people, extended credit where it shouldn't have been given. When creditors came calling, we lost everything – our home, our possessions, our standing in society. He took his own life shortly thereafter, leaving my mother and me to fend for ourselves." Tobias paused, taking a sip of wine to steady himself. The rich flavour flooded his mouth, a luxury he had almost forgotten. "She found work as a companion to an elderly widow, and I... well, I took what employment I could find. My education qualified me for better positions, but without proper references or connections, doors that might once have opened remained firmly closed."

"I'm sorry for your loss," Ritchie said, and seemed to mean it, his expression softening momentarily. "And your mother now?"

"She passed last winter. Influenza." The words were simple but cost him effort to speak. The memory of her final days in that cold, damp room, his inability to provide proper medical care or comfort, remained a wound that had not yet healed.

Ritchie nodded slowly, his eyes never leaving Tobias' face. "So you're alone in the world."

"Yes," Tobias confirmed, wondering why that fact seemed to please his host, whose expression had shifted subtly to something akin to satisfaction.

"As am I," Ritchie said quietly, a certain weight to the words that suggested depths of solitude beyond what Tobias could comprehend. "Though I've had considerably more time to accustom myself to solitude."

The conversation continued through several more courses, none of which Ritchie touched, though he kept Tobias' wine glass full with attentive precision. The food was exquisite – tender meats, vegetables prepared with herbs Tobias couldn't identify, pastries that melted on his tongue. Each dish arrived and departed with perfect timing, served by servants who appeared and disappeared like ghosts, speaking only when necessary.

They spoke of books – Tobias was pleasantly surprised to discover that his new employer shared his love of poetry, particularly the romantics whose celebration of emotion over reason had always resonated with him – and music, and the history of Ruehaven. Ritchie proved to be a captivating conversationalist, his knowledge spanning subjects and eras with an ease that suggested extensive education and experience. Yet he listened as well, seeming genuinely interested in Tobias' opinions and perspectives despite their difference in station.

It was only when dessert arrived – a confection of dark chocolate and raspberries that looked too artful to eat – that Ritchie steered the conversation in an unexpected direction, his posture changing almost imperceptibly.

"I couldn't help but notice something curious about your situation at the stables, Tobias," he said, his voice taking on a subtly different quality that made Tobias' skin prickle with awareness. "Something that set you apart from the typical victim of circumstance."

Tobias set down his fork, suddenly less interested in the dessert and more focused on the shift in Ritchie's demeanour. "Oh?"

"Yes. When I found you being mistreated by those men, there was fear in your eyes, certainly. Anger too. Both natural responses to abuse." Ritchie leaned forward slightly, the candlelight catching the unusual depths in his eyes. "But there was something else – something that caught my attention and held it. A complexity to your reaction that intrigued me."

Tobias remained silent, his heart beginning to beat faster. He had a terrible suspicion about where this conversation might be heading, a direction that both terrified and thrilled him.

"There was a certain... response to your degradation. A flush to your skin that wasn't entirely due to exertion or embarrassment. A dilation of your pupils that suggested something beyond simple distress."

Tobias felt his face grow hot with shame and recognition. He lowered his gaze to the table, unable to meet Ritchie's penetrating stare. "I don't know what you mean," he lied.

"I think you do," Ritchie countered softly, no judgment in his tone, only a certainty that brooked no denial. "Tell me, Tobias. In those moments when they pushed you down, when they tore your clothing and mocked you... did you find, perhaps, a strange sort of pleasure in your humiliation? A secret thrill in being overpowered?"

The question hung in the air between them, dangerous and alluring in equal measure. Tobias stared into his wine glass, watching the play of light through the ruby liquid, his heart pounding against his ribs like a caged bird seeking escape. No one had ever named this shameful secret of his, let alone asked him directly about it. The exposure felt both violating and oddly liberating.

"I... that's absurd," he attempted, but his denial sounded unconvincing even to his own ears, lacking the indignation that true innocence would have mustered.

"There's no judgment here," Ritchie assured him, his voice gentle yet persistent. "Only curiosity. And perhaps recognition of a kindred spirit."

Tobias looked up sharply at that, surprise momentarily overcoming his embarrassment. "What do you mean?"

Ritchie's smile was enigmatic, revealing as little or as much as he chose. He took a moment before responding, as though carefully selecting his words. "There are desires society deems unacceptable, Tobias. Hungers that must be hidden from public view. Longings that most dare not name even to themselves." He paused, his gaze holding Tobias' with hypnotic intensity. "I have lived long enough to recognise that such desires are far more common than most would admit – and that when pursued consensually, between parties who understand and respect each other's needs, they can bring extraordinary fulfilment."

The words resonated within Tobias, striking chords he had long tried to silence. The idea that his shameful yearnings might not be unnatural aberrations but rather aspects of human nature that others shared – that Ritchie himself might share – was both shocking and profoundly relieving.

"And you think... you believe I have such desires?" Tobias managed, his voice barely above a whisper, as though speaking too loudly might shatter this fragile moment of potential understanding.

"I know you do. Just as I know I possess complementary ones." Ritchie's gaze held his, unwavering. "You find a peculiar thrill in submission, in being controlled. In surrendering your will to someone stronger, someone you trust to guide that surrender. I find a similar satisfaction in dominance, in bending another to my will. In accepting the responsibility that comes with another's willing surrender."

The words should have horrified Tobias, should have sent him fleeing from the table and the castle without a backward glance. Such frank discussion of forbidden desires violated every social convention he had been raised to respect. Instead, he felt a shiver of recognition – of relief, even, at having his secret named so plainly, without disgust or condemnation.

"Is that why you brought me here?" he asked, finding unexpected courage in the sanctuary of honest conversation. "To... to indulge these complementary desires?"

"Partly," Ritchie admitted, making no attempt to disguise his interest. "Though I won't deny there's something about you specifically that called to me. A connection I haven't felt in... a very long time."

The way he lingered on those final words suggested a time span beyond what Tobias could comprehend, adding to the growing sense that Ritchie was not quite what he appeared to be.

Tobias took a long swallow of wine, needing its courage to continue this dangerous conversation. The alcohol had begun to warm his blood, loosening the tight constraints of propriety and caution. "And if I were interested in exploring such possibilities? What would that entail?"

"That would depend entirely on our mutual boundaries and consent," Ritchie replied, his voice taking on a formal quality that suggested this was not a subject he took lightly. "I have no interest in unwilling submission, Tobias. True power exchange requires trust and clear communication. I would need to know your limits, your fears, your desires. And you would need to know mine."

"You speak as though you've done this

before." It wasn't quite a question, but the implication was clear.

A shadow passed over Ritchie's face, a fleeting expression of what might have been grief or simply ancient memory. "I have. Though not for many years."

"And what happened to your previous... assistants?" Tobias chose the euphemism deliberately, allowing both of them the pretence that they were still discussing employment.

"They moved on, as all mortals eventually do." Ritchie's expression remained carefully neutral, but there was something in his choice of words that sent another chill through Tobias.

There was that strange phrasing again, the subtle hints that Ritchie was somehow set apart from ordinary men. The rumours from Ruehaven echoed in Tobias' mind with renewed significance – whispers of the castle's master who never aged, who was only seen after sunset, who had inhabited the estate for longer than anyone could remember. Stories told around tavern fires of servants who bore curious marks upon their necks, who became pale and secretive after entering his service.

"What are you?" Tobias asked suddenly, the question escaping before he could reconsider it. The wine had made him bold, perhaps unwisely so.

Ritchie's expression remained unchanged, but something flickered in his eyes – surprise, perhaps, at Tobias' directness, or appreciation for his perspicacity.

"I think you've already guessed," he replied after a moment, neither confirming nor denying the unspoken suspicion that hung between them. "The real question is whether it matters to you."

Tobias considered this, turning the question over in his mind with unexpected clarity despite the wine. If the rumours were true – if Ritchie was indeed what the whispers claimed – then he was sitting across from a creature of myth, a predator by nature. A being who had walked through centuries while others lived and died around him, who sustained himself through means most would consider monstrous.

And yet, this predator had shown him nothing but courtesy and honesty thus far. Had rescued him from abuse, offered him shelter and comfort, and spoken to him as an equal despite the vast gulf between their stations – between their very natures, if the truth was what Tobias suspected.

"It should matter," Tobias said slowly, measuring each word. "By all logic and reason, it should terrify me. I should be making excuses to leave this table, looking for the nearest exit, preparing to flee at first light."

"But?" Ritchie prompted, the single word laden with possibility.

"But I find that it doesn't. Not as much as it should." Tobias met Ritchie's gaze directly, surprised by his own steadiness. "Perhaps because whatever you are, you've treated me with more respect in these few hours than I've received in years as a supposedly ordinary man among my own kind."

Ritchie's smile returned, wider this time, revealing the barest hint of elongated canines that confirmed what Tobias had already intuited. "Then perhaps we have more to discuss."

The revelation should have been shocking, but instead felt like the final piece of a puzzle falling into place. It explained the coldness of Ritchie's touch, his strange phrasing about mortals. It explained why he had not touched the food, why he had appeared at dusk, why the castle staff moved with such practiced discretion.

As the candles burned lower and the night deepened around them, Tobias found himself crossing a threshold he hadn't known existed – stepping willingly into a darkness that promised both danger and deliverance. The wine loosened his tongue further, allowing him to ask questions he would never have dared while sober, to express desires he had never acknowledged aloud.

And as Ritchie outlined the parameters of what could exist between them – a relationship of power and submission, of mutual need and fulfilment, bound by consent and honour – Tobias realised with a strange clarity that he had been waiting for this moment his entire life.

Not just for salvation from poverty and abuse, but for permission to embrace the desires he had always denied – and for someone strong enough to guide him safely through their fulfilment. Someone who understood the complex interplay of pleasure and pain, of surrender and control. Someone who had the strength and experience to accept the gift of his submission without abusing it.

Whether that someone was human or other seemed suddenly less important than the recognition Tobias saw in those ancient eyes – the promise that here, finally, was one who saw him completely and did not turn away.

Chapter Four

Three weeks after arriving at Caldwell Castle, Tobias stood in Ritchie's study, meticulously organising correspondence as part of his official duties as personal assistant. The tall, arched windows were covered with heavy velvet curtains despite the early evening hour – one of many accommodations for his employer's unique condition that Tobias had quickly learnt to accept without question. The rich mahogany desk beneath his fingertips gleamed in the warm glow of oil lamps that cast dancing shadows across the book-lined walls.

The revelation of Ritchie's true nature had come gradually over those first days. No dramatic confession had been necessary; the evidence accumulated naturally through careful observation: the consistent absence of food at Ritchie's place settings during formal meals, his exclusively nocturnal activities and appointments, the preternatural strength he occasionally displayed without apparent thought or effort, the strange, almost hypnotic influence he could exert over others when he chose to do so. Each peculiarity added another piece to the puzzle Tobias was assembling in his mind.

Vampire. The word had never been spoken aloud between them, as if naming it might somehow shatter the delicate understanding they had built, disturbing the careful equilibrium of their relationship. Yet it hung in the air nonetheless.

Strangely, this knowledge had only deepened Tobias' fascination rather than inspiring the fear one might expect. There was something undeniably compelling about Ritchie's ancient eyes, which sometimes reflected centuries of experience in unguarded moments, about the controlled power evident in his every movement, whether turning a page or crossing a room. In his previous life – a life that now seemed distant and foreign – Tobias might have been horrified by such an attraction to darkness. Now, he found it strangely liberating to finally acknowledge the shadowed desires within himself that resonated with Ritchie's own nature.

Their professional relationship had developed smoothly enough. Tobias proved himself both capable and diligent, bringing order to Ritchie's previously neglected affairs with an efficiency that earned the vampire's approving nods and occasional words of praise. But it was their personal interactions that had transformed most dramatically, evolving with a speed that might have been alarming had it not felt so inexplicably right.

The heavy oak door to the study opened with barely a whisper, and Ritchie entered, moving with that fluid grace that still captivated Tobias' attention no matter how often he witnessed it. He wore a simple black shirt of finest silk, open at the collar to reveal the pale column of his throat, and fitted trousers that emphasised his lean strength without appearing deliberately provocative. His dark hair fell loosely around a face that seemed both youthful and ancient simultaneously – a contradiction that Tobias found endlessly fascinating.

"How goes the cataloguing?" Ritchie

enquired, approaching the desk where Tobias worked, his footsteps silent against the ornate carpet.

"Nearly complete, my Lord," Tobias replied, deliberately using the formal address despite their private setting and the late hour. He had quickly learnt that such small acts of deference pleased Ritchie, particularly in the evening hours when the vampire's dominant nature seemed to intensify with the deepening night.

Ritchie's lips curved in subtle acknowledgment of the gesture, a ghost of a smile that transformed his austere features momentarily. "Excellent. And did you complete the other task I assigned you?" His voice carried that particular timbre that always seemed to resonate directly with Tobias' spine.

Tobias felt heat rise to his cheeks, colouring them with a flush he knew Ritchie could perceive even in the room's dim lighting. The "other task" had nothing to do with correspondence or estate management and everything to do with the evolving dynamic between them – a dynamic that existed parallel to but separate from their employer-employee relationship. That morning, before retiring to his chambers as dawn threatened the horizon, Ritchie had instructed Tobias to reflect on their most recent encounter and write down what aspects had affected him most deeply, what sensations had lingered in his memory like persistent echoes.

"Yes, my Lord," Tobias said, his voice dropping slightly, becoming intimate without conscious intent. From inside his waistcoat, he withdrew a carefully folded piece of paper, the creases precise and deliberate, as though the act of folding had been a ritual in itself.

Ritchie took it, his cool fingers brushing against the warmth of Tobias' hand in a contact that sent a familiar shiver through the younger man's body – a reaction impossible to suppress and, he suspected, one that Ritchie intentionally provoked. The vampire unfolded the paper with a deliberate slowness and read its contents, his expression revealing nothing of his thoughts, maintaining that perfect control that Tobias had come to both admire and crave.

Their transition from employer and employee to dominant and submissive had progressed with careful deliberation that belied the intensity underlying it. After their candid dinner conversation that first night, Ritchie had given Tobias time to consider what such a relationship might entail – days of subtle glances and carefully worded questions that tested boundaries without fully crossing them. When Tobias had finally indicated his willingness to explore further, gathering his courage one evening as they sat before the library fire, Ritchie had established clear parameters – rules and expectations that would govern their interactions when they stepped into those roles together.

What had followed was an education unlike any Tobias could have imagined possible outside his most private fantasies. Ritchie proved to be a demanding but attentive dominant, one who took as much pleasure in Tobias' responses as in his own exercise of control. Their sessions together were carefully orchestrated exercises in power exchange, with Ritchie systematically dismantling Tobias' composed exterior through a combination of psychological dominance and physical control that left him simultaneously vulnerable and exhilarated.

Yet there had been no intimacy of the conventional sort – no hasty couplings or desperate embraces. Ritchie seemed more interested in Tobias' emotional responses than his physical form – in breaking down his defences and reducing him to his most vulnerable state, stripped of pretence and protection. The humiliation and degradation that had once been haphazardly inflicted by crude stable hands was now precisely administered by a master of the craft, calibrated with exquisite care to push Tobias to his limits without breaking him, like a musician coaxing complex harmonies from a perfectly tuned instrument.

"Interesting," Ritchie murmured, folding the paper with the same deliberate care with which it had been originally creased, before slipping it into his own pocket rather than returning it – a small assertion of ownership that did not go unnoticed. "You continue to surprise me with your self-awareness, Tobias. Many take years to understand their own desires as clearly as you have articulated them here."

"Thank you, my Lord." The praise settled warmly in Tobias' chest, sparking a satisfaction deeper than any conventional compliment could evoke.

Ritchie circled the desk with predatory grace, coming to stand directly behind Tobias, close enough that Tobias could sense his presence without turning, could almost feel the cool aura that surrounded the vampire like an invisible mantle. "Your work has been exemplary today. Every task completed with attention to detail that I find... most gratifying. I believe you've earned a reward."

The words sent a pulse of anticipation through Tobias, quickening his breath and heightening his awareness of every sensation – the slight pressure of his clothing against his skin, the warmth of the fire across the room, the faint scent of ink and paper that permeated the study. In their established dynamic, rewards were often more challenging than punishments – opportunities for Tobias to surrender more completely, to embrace desires he still struggled to accept in the light of day, when rationality threatened to overcome instinct.

"Look at me," Ritchie commanded softly, his voice carrying that subtle undercurrent of power that made refusal unthinkable.

Tobias turned, finding himself mere inches from the vampire, close enough to observe the minute details of his features – the perfect symmetry that humans could approach but never achieve, the unblemished skin that testified to his separation from mortality's ravages. Ritchie's eyes had taken on the faintest crimson tinge around the iris – a sign of hunger or arousal or perhaps both inextricably entwined.

"Three weeks you've been in my home," Ritchie observed, reaching out to trace the line of Tobias' jaw with one finger, the touch cool but not cold, firm but not harsh. "Three weeks of learning each other's boundaries and desires. Three weeks of building trust through small surrenders and controlled tests. I believe it's time we deepen our connection in a way unique to what I am."

There was no mistaking his meaning, no possibility of misinterpreting the intent behind his words. Though they had never discussed it directly, never approached the subject even in their most intimate exchanges, Tobias had wondered when this moment would come – when Ritchie would finally seek to taste his blood, to consummate their relationship in the manner most fundamental to his nature.

"Are you afraid?" Ritchie asked, his voice gentle despite the predatory gleam in his eyes, a dichotomy that summarised much about him.

Tobias considered the question seriously, searching his feelings beneath the immediate physical responses of his body. "Not of you," he answered truthfully, meeting Ritchie's gaze directly. "Perhaps of what it means. Of what I'll become by allowing it – by taking this step that cannot be untaken."

Ritchie's expression softened slightly, appreciation for the honest answer evident in the relaxation of his features. "Perceptive as always. The physical act itself is merely an exchange of fluid and sensation, no different in principle from many others. The psychological significance, however..." He let the thought hang unfinished between them, allowing Tobias to contemplate its implications.

"Will it change me?" Tobias asked, voicing the concern that had lingered at the edges of his consciousness since he'd first recognised Ritchie's nature. "Physically, I mean." The legends and folklore surrounding vampires were abundant and contradictory, and he had no way to distinguish truth from fiction without asking directly.

"Not from a single feeding, no," Ritchie assured him, his tone matter-of-fact rather than condescending. "It takes far more than that to transform a human – multiple exchanges over time, with intent behind them. But it will create a connection between us that transcends the merely physical. My bite carries a certain... influence. A pleasure unlike any you've experienced, different in quality from what our other activities have provided."

Tobias swallowed, his pulse quickening visibly in his throat – a reaction he knew Ritchie could both see and hear with his enhanced senses. The thought was both intimidating and exciting in equal measure. "And is that what you want? To influence me? To have that power over me?" The question wasn't accusatory but genuinely curious.

"I want your submission freely given," Ritchie

replied, his hand now cupping Tobias' cheek in a gesture that managed to be both possessive and tender simultaneously. "The influence is temporary, a physiological response rather than a permanent alteration of your will. But the memory of it will remain, becoming part of the foundation we build together. The choice, as always, is yours. I will not take what is not offered willingly."

In truth, it hardly felt like a choice at all, but rather the inevitable next step in a journey they had begun the moment their paths crossed. From the moment Ritchie had assisted him from the hay-strewn floor of Whitfield's stable, Tobias had been moving towards this point, drawn by forces he could name but not fully comprehend. Each step in their evolving relationship had only deepened his desire to surrender completely to the dark attraction between them, to embrace the shadow rather than merely acknowledging it.

"Yes. Please," Tobias whispered, the word carrying all the weight of a vow, simple but profound in its commitment. "This is what I want."

Ritchie's eyes flashed with satisfaction, the crimson tinge momentarily intensifying before subsiding. "Remove your shirt and wait for me by the fireplace," he instructed, his voice taking on the commanding tone that marked their transition into their established roles.

Tobias complied without hesitation, fingers working at the small pearl buttons of his waistcoat and then the finer ones of his linen shirt until both garments hung open, revealing the pale skin beneath that glowed golden in the firelight. He moved with deliberate steps to the large fireplace where flames crackled merrily among seasoned logs, providing the room's primary illumination. The warmth against his exposed skin was a pleasant contrast to the castle's perpetual chill, which seemed to permeate even the thick stone walls.

Behind him, he heard Ritchie moving about the room – the soft clink of crystal against crystal, the liquid sound of wine being poured from decanter to glass. Then the vampire was beside him again, appearing with that uncanny silence that still occasionally startled Tobias despite his growing accustomed to it. Ritchie held two crystal glasses containing a deep red liquid that caught the firelight like liquid rubies.

"Wine?" Tobias asked, accepting the glass offered to him, his fingers careful not to touch Ritchie's until permission for such contact was granted.

"For you, yes – a particularly fine Bordeaux from my cellars. For me, something more sustaining from my private stock. A ritual before we proceed, to mark the significance of this moment." Ritchie raised his glass in a formal toast. "To boundaries crossed and desires fulfilled, to darkness embraced rather than feared."

They drank, the rich wine warming Tobias from within, its complex notes of blackberry and oak spreading across his tongue as he savoured it, fortifying him for what was to come. When he had drained his glass, Ritchie took it from him and set both vessels aside on a small table inlaid with mother-of-pearl that gleamed iridescently in the flickering light.

"Remove your shirt completely," the vampire

instructed, his voice taking on the commanding tone that never failed to send a shiver of anticipation through Tobias' body, awakening responses he had once tried to suppress but now embraced fully.

Once again, Tobias obeyed without hesitation, shrugging off the garments and standing bare-chested in the firelight that highlighted the contours of his torso, casting some areas in warm illumination while leaving others in shadow. Though they had progressed to partial nudity in previous sessions, exploring the vulnerability such exposure created, there was a different quality to the moment now – a sense of ritual and significance that made each action feel weighted with meaning.

Ritchie circled him slowly, appraisingly, like a connoisseur evaluating a fine statue, occasionally reaching out to trace a finger along Tobias' skin – across the breadth of his shoulders, down the subtle ridge of his spine, around to the hollow of his throat where his pulse beat visibly. Each touch left a trail of goosebumps in its wake, a physical manifestation of the effect Ritchie had on him even with the most casual contact.

"Beautiful," Ritchie murmured, the word carrying no hint of mockery despite its potential to humiliate if delivered differently. "You've filled out since you arrived. Good food and proper rest have restored what deprivation took from you, returning the vitality that is your natural state."

"Thanks to your generosity, my Lord," Tobias responded, genuinely grateful for the care that had been taken of him since his arrival – a stark contrast to his previous circumstances.

"Not generosity," Ritchie corrected, though without harshness. "Investment. Everything I've given you has been in service to this moment – to having you stand before me, strong and vital, offering yourself willingly rather than from desperation or coercion. Genuine submission requires strength, not weakness."

The words should have been offensive, reducing their relationship to a transaction, a calculated exchange of resources for services. Instead, Tobias found them strangely arousing – an honest acknowledgment of Ritchie's predatory nature and his own willing participation in it. There was a purity to the exchange, a clarity of purpose that made it feel more meaningful, not less.

"Kneel," Ritchie commanded, gesturing to the space before him.

Tobias sank to his knees on the thick carpet, his posture straight as Ritchie had taught him during previous sessions, shoulders back to display his chest, head neither lowered in false modesty nor raised in challenge, hands resting palms-up on his thighs – the position of offering they had practiced, symbolising his willingness to give and receive according to Ritchie's direction.

Ritchie stood before him, tall and imposing from this lower vantage point, one hand coming to rest in Tobias' hair, fingers tangling in the blond strands that had grown longer since his arrival at the castle. "Do you know why I chose you, Tobias?"

"No, my Lord," Tobias answered truthfully, curiosity mingling with the anticipation already coursing through him.

"Because from the moment I saw you, even

in those degraded circumstances, I recognised something in you that mirrored something in myself – a hunger for experiences beyond the mundane, beyond what ordinary existence could provide. A willingness to embrace the darkness rather than fear it, to seek pleasure in places others would never dare explore." Ritchie's grip tightened slightly, the mild discomfort focusing Tobias' attention completely on his words. "In centuries of existence, moving among countless humans, I have rarely encountered such perfect complementarity – such potential for mutual satisfaction."

The praise washed over Tobias like warm honey, sinking into his very core where it dissolved the last lingering doubts he had harboured. Throughout his life, he had felt like an aberration – his desires shameful secrets to be hidden away lest they invite rejection or worse. To have them not merely accepted but celebrated by someone who understood them completely, who saw them as valuable rather than perverse, was a liberation he had never dared hope for, even in his most optimistic moments.

"Thank you, my Lord," he whispered, eyes

lowered in genuine gratitude that went beyond the formality of their roles.

"Look at me," Ritchie commanded, and Tobias raised his gaze to meet the vampire's, finding his eyes now unmistakably rimmed with crimson. "What I take from you tonight, I do not take lightly or casually. Your blood is a gift I will honour, not merely consume. Remember that, whatever you may feel in the moments to come."

With that, Ritchie pulled Tobias to his feet with effortless strength and guided him towards the high-backed leather chair positioned near the fire. Seating himself with regal grace, the vampire positioned Tobias to stand between his knees, then pulled him down with gentle insistence until the young man was seated sideways across his lap – an intimate position that left Tobias feeling both vulnerable and strangely protected, cradled against Ritchie's solid form.

"Relax," Ritchie murmured, one arm circling Tobias' waist to support him while the other hand tilted his head to expose the side of his neck where the pulse beat visibly beneath the fair skin. "Trust me to give you what you need, what we both need from this exchange."

Tobias forced his tense muscles to loosen one by one, consciously slowing his breathing despite the frantic beating of his heart that refused to be calmed by rational thought. He felt Ritchie's lips against his skin first – cool and soft, pressing gentle kisses along the column of his throat that seemed designed to both soothe and heighten anticipation simultaneously. Then came the sharp scrape of fangs, testing but not yet breaking the skin, sending electric pulses of sensation through his body that made him gasp.

"Please," Tobias heard himself say, the word escaping him involuntarily, though he couldn't articulate exactly what he was asking for, even to himself. More pressure? Release from the exquisite tension building between them? Or simply for Ritchie to take what they both knew he needed, completing the exchange that had been building towards this moment?

"Patience," Ritchie whispered against his skin, his breath cool compared to the heat radiating from Tobias' body. "I've waited weeks for this moment, cultivating it carefully. I intend to savour it rather than rushing to completion too quickly. The anticipation is part of the pleasure, for both of us." The vampire's hand slid up Tobias' bare chest to rest over his heart, feeling its rapid rhythm beneath his palm like a bird struggling against confinement. "Your anticipation is intoxicating, a complex bouquet of fear and desire so perfectly balanced, neither overpowering the other but creating something greater than either alone."

"I'm not afraid," Tobias protested weakly, though the tremor in his voice betrayed the statement's partial untruth.

"No?" Ritchie's lips curved against his neck in what Tobias could feel was a smile, though he couldn't see it from his position. "Then what makes your heart race so wildly beneath my hand? What sends this tremor through your body when I touch you here?" His fingers trailed along Tobias' collarbone, demonstrating the shiver that followed his touch. "There is no shame in fear, Tobias. It is the natural response to power greater than one's own. The courage lies in facing it rather than fleeing from it."

Before Tobias could formulate a response to this observation, Ritchie's fangs pierced his skin without further warning – a sharp, bright pain that made him gasp aloud, his body tensing momentarily before Ritchie's arm tightened around him, holding him securely. But the pain transformed almost immediately, dissolving like sugar in hot water, replaced by waves of pleasure that radiated from the point of penetration throughout his entire body, reaching even his fingertips and toes with tingling intensity.

Tobias felt his head fall back against Ritchie's shoulder, surrendering to the sensation, a deep moan escaping his lips as the vampire began to drink in earnest. Each pull of Ritchie's mouth against his neck sent another surge of sensation through him – pleasure unlike anything he had experienced before, as promised. It was beyond physical, touching something deeper, more primal, that existed beneath conscious thought or rational understanding.

Ritchie's arm tightened around him, supporting his increasingly limp body as the feeding continued and Tobias surrendered more completely to the experience. Through the haze of pleasure that clouded his thoughts, Tobias sensed Ritchie's own satisfaction and pleasure – felt it in the tension of the vampire's body against his own, heard it in the soft sounds of appreciation that vibrated against his throat where Ritchie's lips remained sealed to his skin.

Time seemed to stretch and contract simultaneously, losing all meaning as normal perception altered. Tobias lost all sense of how long they remained locked together in their intimate exchange, inseparable as the physical boundary between them blurred through the sharing of his essence. He only knew that when Ritchie finally withdrew his fangs with careful deliberation, gently licking the wounds closed with meticulous attention, he felt a profound sense of loss and emptiness that was almost painful in its intensity.

"Breathe," Ritchie instructed softly, one hand stroking Tobias' hair with unexpected tenderness as the young man struggled to reorient himself to normal consciousness after the transcendent experience. "Slowly and deeply. Let your body remember its rhythms."

Tobias obeyed without thinking, drawing deep breaths that gradually cleared the pleasant fog from his mind and restored some strength to his limbs. He felt strangely light, as though gravity had less hold on him than before, his body weightless against Ritchie's supporting form.

"Are you alright?" Ritchie asked, genuine concern evident in his voice, a momentary break from his usual controlled demeanour that Tobias recognised as significant even in his current state.

"Yes," Tobias managed, his own voice sounding distant and strange to his ears, as though it belonged to someone else. "That was... I didn't expect... I couldn't have imagined..."

"The intensity?" Ritchie supplied when words failed him. "Few do, their first time. The legends speak of pain and terror, rarely of pleasure. It serves my kind to maintain such misconceptions."

"Will it always feel like that?" Tobias asked, unable to imagine experiencing such overwhelming sensation repeatedly and surviving with his sanity intact.

A small smile played at Ritchie's lips, now tinged slightly red with Tobias' blood – a sight that should have been horrifying but instead struck Tobias as strangely intimate, a visual representation of their shared experience. "Each time is different, influenced by the emotional state of both participants, the circumstances surrounding the exchange. But yes, there is always pleasure – a biological mechanism evolved to ensure willing donors, I suppose. Nature's way of facilitating the relationship between predator and prey."

The practical explanation should have diminished the experience, reducing it to mere biology, to chemical reactions and evolutionary adaptations devoid of deeper meaning. Instead, Tobias found himself grateful for Ritchie's honesty – for treating him as a partner worthy of truth rather than a victim to be deceived with pretty lies or romantic distortions of reality.

"Thank you," Tobias said softly, meaning far more than the words could adequately express. "For sharing this with me. For allowing me to experience what few humans ever do."

Ritchie studied him for a long moment, something unreadable in his ancient eyes that had now returned to their normal state, the crimson tinge having faded with the satisfaction of his hunger. "In my long existence, I have taken blood from countless humans – some willing, many not, particularly in my earlier years when control was more difficult to maintain. But it has been... a very long time since I've felt such satisfaction in the exchange, such perfect alignment of desire and fulfilment." His thumb brushed over Tobias' lower lip in an intimate gesture. "Your submission honours me, Tobias Marlow. Never doubt that."

The formal acknowledgment, the use of his full name, sent a warm glow through Tobias' chest that spread outward, filling the curious emptiness left by the feeding with something equally powerful but different in nature. He felt changed by the experience, though not in the physical way he had initially feared. Something fundamental had shifted between them – a deepening of their connection that transcended their established roles as dominant and submissive, employer and employee, vampire and human. They had crossed a threshold together into territory neither could fully return from.

"Rest now," Ritchie said, helping Tobias to his feet with careful attention to his slightly unsteady balance. "The first feeding can be draining in more ways than the obvious. I've taken only a modest amount, but your body needs time to recover, to replenish what has been given."

"Will you join me?" Tobias asked, surprising himself with his boldness, with the implied invitation that went beyond anything they had previously shared.

Ritchie's expression softened, a genuine tenderness briefly visible beneath his usual controlled exterior. "Not tonight. The feeding heightens certain... appetites that are best indulged separately for now, until you're more accustomed to my nature and its implications." He pressed a gentle kiss to Tobias' forehead – a gesture of affection rather than passion. "Go. Sleep. We'll speak more tomorrow evening, when you've had time to process what has occurred between us."

As Tobias made his way back to his chambers through the silent corridors of the castle, he felt the dual puncture wounds on his neck with tentative fingers, exploring their texture with a mixture of wonder and disbelief. They had already closed completely, leaving only a slight tenderness to mark their existence – physical evidence of a boundary crossed that could never be uncrossed, of a surrender more complete than any he had offered before.

In the solitude of his bed, as drowsiness pulled him irresistibly towards sleep – a natural reaction to the blood loss, he supposed, however minimal Ritchie had claimed it to be – Tobias realised with perfect clarity that he had finally found what he had unconsciously sought his entire life: acceptance of his darkest desires without judgment or condemnation, and someone strong enough to meet them without hesitation or compromise.

For the first time since arriving at Caldwell Castle, Tobias slept without dreams or nightmares, wrapped in the strange peace that comes from embracing one's true nature, whatever its shadows might hold. Tomorrow would bring new challenges, new expectations, new boundaries to explore – but tonight, in this moment, everything was exactly as it should be.

Chapter Five

As autumn deepened into winter, Caldwell Castle became a world unto itself, isolated from Ruehaven by frequent snowstorms and the increasingly shorter days. The ancient stone walls now seemed to draw inward against the biting cold, creating a sanctuary of shadow and silence. Frozen landscapes stretched in every direction, the pristine white snow reflecting the pale moonlight that cast long, ethereal shadows across the castle grounds. For Ritchie, the extended darkness was a blessing, allowing him greater freedom of movement beyond the confines of his chambers. The lengthening nights meant more hours to roam the sprawling corridors, to exist without the constant awareness of the sun's position in the sky. For Tobias, the isolation only intensified his focus on the relationship that had come to define his existence, his thoughts increasingly consumed by the enigmatic being with whom he now shared this secluded world.

Their dynamic had evolved rapidly after that first feeding. What began as carefully negotiated scenes of dominance and submission transformed into a continuous exchange of power that permeated every aspect of their interaction. The structured boundaries that had initially defined their encounters gradually dissolved, replaced by an unspoken understanding that transcended formal arrangement. Ritchie no longer needed to issue explicit commands; a look or gesture was sufficient to communicate his expectations – a raised eyebrow, a slight tilt of his head, the subtle positioning of his body within a room. And Tobias found himself anticipating those expectations, his sensitivity to Ritchie's moods and desires growing more acute with each passing day. He began to recognise the almost imperceptible shifts in Ritchie's demeanour that signalled hunger, desire, or displeasure, his body responding instinctively before his mind fully processed the cues.

The feedings, too, had become regular occurrences – weekly rituals that both men anticipated with increasing hunger, a ceremony of intimacy that punctuated the rhythm of their shared existence. The anticipation would build as the appointed day approached, charging the air between them with an electric tension that heightened every interaction. For Tobias, the bite had become a reward more potent than any praise, a moment of transcendence that he craved with an intensity that sometimes frightened him. In the hours before each feeding, he found himself distracted, his skin hypersensitive, his thoughts scattered like leaves before a gathering storm. The memory of previous feedings would replay in his mind – the exquisite pressure of fangs breaking skin, the initial sharp pain that flowered into overwhelming pleasure, the dizzying sensation of blood being drawn from his body into Ritchie's.

It was during one such feeding, as December's first heavy snow blanketed the castle grounds in hushed stillness, that Tobias began to understand the true nature of his descent. Outside, the world had transformed into a monochrome painting of white and shadow, the familiar landscape rendered strange and new beneath its frozen covering. Inside, a transformation of a different kind was taking place – one less visible but no less profound.

They were in Ritchie's private chambers – a rare privilege that had only recently been extended to him, an intimate boundary crossed that signified the deepening of their connection. Unlike the rest of the castle, with its gothic grandeur and historical furnishings, Ritchie's personal space was surprisingly modern and minimal. Clean lines and sparse decoration created an atmosphere of timeless elegance that somehow managed to complement rather than clash with the castle's ancient architecture. The massive bed was the room's focal point, its dark sheets a stark contrast to the pale walls, the simplicity of the space highlighting the luxury of the few carefully chosen pieces that adorned it. A single painting hung opposite the bed – an abstract study in crimson and black that seemed to pulse with its own internal rhythm in the flickering firelight.

Tobias lay back against the pillows, his shirt discarded on the floor where Ritchie had carelessly tossed it, his skin prickling with goosebumps that owed more to anticipation than to the room's temperature. The fire in the hearth cast dancing shadows across his exposed torso, illuminating the slight marks from previous feedings that had not completely faded – a constellation of pale scars that mapped the progression of their relationship. Ritchie knelt beside him, his presence commanding even in this position of apparent supplication. The vampire's eyes gleamed crimson in the firelight, reflecting the flames like polished garnets, his desire unconcealed in a gaze that seemed to penetrate beyond flesh to the rushing blood beneath.

"You've been distracted today," Ritchie observed, one cool hand tracing patterns on Tobias' chest, fingertips following the contours of muscle and bone with deliberate precision. The touch was light enough to tease yet firm enough to assert control, a physical reminder of the power dynamic that defined their relationship despite its evolution. "Your mind wandering during our conversation about the estate accounts. The numbers clearly failed to hold your attention."

"I apologise, my Lord," Tobias replied

automatically, the formality of address slipping out despite their current intimacy. His breath caught as Ritchie's fingers skimmed across a particularly sensitive spot just below his collarbone. "It won't happen again."

Ritchie's fingers stilled, applying the slightest pressure – not quite a warning, but a demand for honesty. "I'm not interested in empty promises, Tobias. I want to know what thoughts pulled you from your duties." The vampire's voice carried centuries of command, soft in volume but unyielding in expectation, leaving no room for prevarication or half-truths.

There was no point in deception; Ritchie would sense any lie, would detect the subtle changes in heartbeat and respiration that betrayed human dishonesty. The vampire's heightened senses made him an infallible detector of falsehood, a fact that had compelled Tobias towards radical honesty from the beginning of their arrangement. "I was thinking about this," Tobias admitted, gesturing vaguely to encompass their current position, the intimate space they occupied together. "About the feeding. About how much I've come to need it." The confession emerged more vulnerable than he had intended, the raw truth of his dependence laid bare between them.

"Need it?" Ritchie repeated, his head tilting slightly. The single eyebrow that arched upward conveyed curiosity tinged with something deeper – perhaps concern, perhaps satisfaction. "An interesting choice of words. Tell me more." The request was gentle but carried the unmistakable weight of command beneath its surface.

Tobias swallowed, struggling to articulate feelings he barely understood himself, to give shape to the formless hunger that had taken root within him. His fingers twisted in the dark sheets, seeking an anchor as he ventured into emotional territory that felt both dangerous and necessary to explore. "At first, it was just pleasure – intense, unlike anything I'd experienced. Something extraordinary but ultimately separate from who I am." He paused, searching for the right words to capture the transformation that had occurred within him. "But lately, it's different. I find myself counting the days between feedings, growing restless as the time approaches. My work suffers, my sleep becomes fitful. I catch myself touching the marks on my neck, reliving the sensation." The admission felt like stepping off a precipice, exhilarating and terrifying in equal measure. "When you finally take from me, it's... it's like everything falls into place. Like the world makes sense again. Like I've been holding my breath for days and can finally exhale."

Ritchie's expression grew serious, the predatory hunger in his eyes tempered by something more contemplative. His gaze travelled over Tobias' face as if seeing him anew, cataloguing subtle changes that might have escaped a less observant witness. "What you're describing sounds like dependence, Tobias," he said finally, the words carrying neither judgment nor approval, merely observation.

"Is that... is that normal?" Tobias asked, uncertainty colouring his voice. He had entered their arrangement with clear expectations about physical pleasure and power exchange, but had never anticipated this profound alteration of his inner landscape, this realignment of his desires around Ritchie's bite.

"It's not uncommon." Ritchie's blunt description contrasted sharply with the intimacy of their position, the frank detachment of his explanation at odds with the heated tension between their bodies. His fingers resumed their exploration of Tobias' chest, tracing the outline of his ribcage with academic precision that nevertheless sent shivers of pleasure across his skin. "It's an evolutionary adaptation, you might say – one that benefits my kind." A ghost of a smile crossed his lips. "But what you're describing goes beyond the typical reaction."

A cold unease settled in Tobias' stomach, displacing some of the desire that had warmed him moments before. The clinical explanation of his feelings as mere biology threatened to undermine the significance he had attributed to their connection. "Are you saying there's something wrong with me?" The question emerged smaller than intended, betraying an insecurity he typically kept well-hidden.

"No," Ritchie said quickly, his hand moving to cup Tobias' cheek in a gesture of reassurance, thumb brushing lightly across his cheekbone. "I'm saying that your natural predisposition towards submission, combined with the effects of my feeding, has created a deeper bond than I anticipated. It's not wrong, but it requires... attention."

"What kind of attention?" Tobias asked, leaning almost imperceptibly into Ritchie's touch, his body betraying the very dependence they were discussing. The warmth of the fire and the intoxicating proximity of the vampire created a cocoon of intimacy around them, making the rest of the world seem distant and inconsequential.

Instead of answering immediately, Ritchie leaned down and pressed his lips to Tobias' in a rare kiss. The contact was brief but sent a shock of pleasure through Tobias' system, making him arch up involuntarily, his body seeking more of the unexpected connection. Ritchie's lips were cooler than a human's would be, but not cold. The kiss carried none of the bloodlust that often characterised their physical interactions, offering instead a different kind of hunger, one that spoke of desire beyond sustenance.

"The kind that acknowledges what's happening between us goes beyond our initial arrangement," Ritchie murmured against his lips, their faces still close enough that Tobias could feel the vibration of each word. "The kind that requires me to be more careful with you than I have been." His eyes studied Tobias with an intensity that seemed to pierce through pretence to the core of his being. "The kind that recognises the responsibility that comes with the power I hold over you."

Despite the warning in Ritchie's words, Tobias felt a thrill at the implication that their connection was exceptional – that he had somehow affected the ancient vampire in unexpected ways. The idea that he, a mortal man of no particular significance, could disrupt the carefully controlled existence of a being who had witnessed centuries unfold was intoxicating in its own right. It offered a sense of power within his submission, a significance that transcended the mundane boundaries of his formerly ordinary life.

"I don't want you to be careful with me," he whispered, emboldened by the admission of their unusual bond. The firelight cast half of Ritchie's face in shadow, emphasising the angles of his features as Tobias reached up to trace the sharp line of his jaw. "I want to give you everything." The words hung in the air between them, laden with implications that extended far beyond the physical offering of his blood.

Something darkened in Ritchie's expression – hunger mixed with what might have been concern, or perhaps regret. His hand captured Tobias' wrist, stilling the exploratory touch with gentle but irresistible force. "You don't understand what you're offering, Tobias," he said, his voice dropping to a register that seemed to resonate directly with Tobias' bones.

"Then help me understand." The request was simple but sincere, an invitation to knowledge that might bridge the vast gulf of experience that separated them – the mere decades of mortal life against centuries of immortal existence.

Ritchie was silent for a long moment, his fingers still holding Tobias' wrist with that gentle but unyielding pressure. When he finally spoke, his voice carried the weight of centuries of experience, each word chosen with deliberate care. "If I were to turn you – and I speak only in hypotheticals – you must understand it would be the most irreversible decision of your existence." His dark eyes searched Tobias' face, as though trying to gauge whether the young man could truly comprehend what he was suggesting. "Transformation is absolute; there is no path back to mortality. No remedy, no cure, no divine intervention that could restore what was lost."

He released Tobias' wrist and rose from the bed to pace the room. The firelight cast his shadow long across the floor, a dark echo of his form. "You speak of giving me everything, but do you understand what 'everything' means? Your daylight hours... gone forever. The simple pleasure of a meal, the satisfaction of ordinary food... replaced by a singular hunger that can never be fully sated. The ability to form connections with mortals... significantly diminished, replaced by the constant awareness of their fragility, their brief lives flickering past like candle flames while you remain unchanged."

He turned back to face Tobias, and there was something ancient and sorrowful in his expression. "I have watched countless mortals age and die – entire bloodlines extinguished while I persist. You think you understand loneliness now, but mortal solitude is nothing compared to the isolation of outliving everyone and everything you might come to care for."

Ritchie returned to the bed, sitting close enough that Tobias could feel the coolness radiating from him. "And then there is the hunger itself. You feel dependent on my bite now, but that is a gentle craving compared to the endless thirst that defines our existence. The constant awareness of every heartbeat around you, the perpetual temptation of warm blood flowing just beneath fragile skin. The discipline required to resist that call, day after day, year after year, century after century – many fail. Many become the monsters of legend, losing themselves to bloodlust."

His hand found Tobias' face again, cradling it with infinite tenderness. "I would not wish that struggle upon you lightly. You are precious to me, Tobias – more than you perhaps realise. And it is because I care for you that I would have you understand the full weight of what transformation means. It is not merely an intensification of what exists between us now. It is a fundamental alteration of your very nature, one that would echo through eternity."

The concept should have terrified Tobias. This erosion of his humanity, this metamorphosis into something other, ought to have triggered every survival instinct, every ingrained fear of the unnatural. Instead, he felt a strange longing unfurl within him, a yearning for the very transformation Ritchie described. To be changed by Ritchie – the idea held a dark appeal that resonated with his deepest desires, desires he had scarcely acknowledged even to himself before this moment.

Tobias sat up slightly, propping himself against the headboard to better observe Ritchie's expression. "Have you... have you done this before? Turned someone, I mean?" The question emerged hesitantly, laden with unacknowledged jealousy at the thought of Ritchie having shared this profound connection with others before him.

Ritchie's expression withdrew slightly, a

shuttering of emotion that Tobias had come to recognise as a defensive reaction. "Yes. Long ago." The brevity of his response suggested reluctance to elaborate, a rare door closed in their increasingly open relationship.

"What happened to them?" Tobias pressed, needing to understand the potential trajectory of the path he was already walking. The room seemed to narrow around them, the outside world fading further as the conversation delved into Ritchie's closely guarded past.

Something like regret flickered across Ritchie's features, there and gone so quickly that Tobias might have imagined it. "She exists still, somewhere in the world. We parted ways over a century ago." The casual mention of the time passed highlighted the vast gulf between their experience: what was ancient history to Tobias remained relatively recent memory for Ritchie.

The revelation that Ritchie had turned another into a vampire, that this unknown female still walked the earth, sparked an unexpected jealousy in Tobias. The emotion flared hot and sudden in his chest, surprising him with its intensity. "Why did you part?" he asked, struggling to keep his voice neutral despite the possessive feeling that had taken hold of him. The irrational sense of betrayal – that Ritchie had shared the ultimate intimacy with another – was all the more unsettling for its unexpectedness.

"Immortality is a long time to spend with another being, no matter how strong the initial connection," Ritchie said simply, though something in his tone suggested the parting had not been as uncomplicated as his words implied. "Eventually, paths diverge. Interests change. The world transforms around you, and you must either transform with it or become a relic of a bygone era." He gestured vaguely towards the window, where the world lay beyond the castle's ancient stones. "She embraced change more readily than I. Her vision of immortality involved constant reinvention, while I preferred to maintain certain... consistencies."

The practical response did little to ease Tobias' sudden discomfort, the unwelcome image of Ritchie with this unnamed woman intruding on his thoughts. He found himself irrationally curious about her appearance, her personality, the nature of their relationship before and after her transformation. "And is that what you expect of me? To eventually become like her? To walk away?" The questions emerged more confrontational than intended, betraying his emotional investment in what had begun as a clinical discussion of supernatural physiology.

Ritchie's hand returned to Tobias' face, thumb stroking his cheekbone with surprising tenderness, the touch seeming to acknowledge the emotional undercurrent of their conversation. "I don't know what I expect of you, Tobias," he admitted, the candour unusual from one normally so controlled in his disclosures. "That's what disturbs me. Over the centuries, I've prided myself on clarity of purpose and decision. I've approached each relationship – feeding or otherwise – with clear boundaries and aims." His gaze fixed on some middle distance, as though seeing through the castle walls to the sequence of vital encounters that had preceded this one. "Yet with you, I find myself... conflicted."

The admission of uncertainty from a being so ancient and powerful was both flattering and unsettling. It suggested that their connection had transcended Ritchie's careful planning, that Tobias had somehow penetrated defences erected over centuries of existence. "Because of what I'm becoming?" he asked, seeking to understand the source of Ritchie's unprecedented indecision.

"Because of what you make me feel," Ritchie corrected quietly, attention returning fully to Tobias with an intensity that made him catch his breath. "Emotions I thought long buried by time. Concerns I believed I had transcended. Desires that extend beyond the pleasure you provide." Each admission seemed reluctantly offered, as though extracted against Ritchie's better judgment by some compulsion neither of them fully understood.

Before Tobias could pursue this revelation, this unprecedented glimpse into Ritchie's inner landscape, the vampire's expression shifted, a decision visibly made. The momentary vulnerability vanished behind the composed mask that Tobias had come to know so well during their early interactions.

"Enough talk," Ritchie said, his tone regaining its customary authority. "You came here for the feeding, and I've kept you waiting."

The abrupt return to their established roles was jarring, but Tobias recognised Ritchie's deflection for what it was – a retreat from vulnerability, a reassertion of control when emotions threatened to expose too much. Rather than press, he tilted his head to expose his neck, offering the submission that had become as natural as breathing. The movement was practiced now, performed with a grace born of repetition, his body remembering the optimal angle to grant Ritchie easiest access to his preferred feeding site.

Ritchie's eyes darkened with hunger, his earlier hesitation apparently forgotten as more primal instincts asserted themselves. The crimson deepened to near-black, pupils dilating until they nearly eclipsed the iris entirely. He leaned down, lips brushing the sensitive skin where neck met shoulder – Tobias' favourite feeding site, as Ritchie well knew. The light contact sent shivers of anticipation down Tobias' spine, his body responding with conditioned eagerness to the promise of what would follow.

The vampire's lips pressed more firmly against Tobias' neck, not quite a kiss but more intimate than mere preparation. Tobias felt his desire intensify, the danger inherent in their exchange only heightening his arousal. "Please," he whispered, the word emerging as both request and demand. "I need it."

The admission of dependency seemed to satisfy something in Ritchie, some need for acknowledgment of the power he wielded. With a low sound that was almost a growl, he sank his fangs into Tobias' flesh, the penetration practiced and precise, finding the optimal spot with unerring accuracy.

The now-familiar pleasure washed over Tobias, radiating outward from the point of connection to suffuse his entire body with warmth. The initial sharp pain transformed almost instantly into waves of ecstasy that surpassed any physical pleasure he had known before their arrangement. His fingers clutched at Ritchie's shoulders, not to push away but to anchor himself against the overwhelming sensation.

But there was something different this time

– a deeper connection, as though some barrier between them had thinned to near-transparency. As Ritchie drank, Tobias felt not only his own pleasure but echoes of Ritchie's satisfaction, creating a feedback loop of sensation that threatened to overwhelm him. The vampire's hunger, his satiation, the complex emotions that accompanied the feeding – all transferred through their connection with unprecedented clarity, adding layers to Tobias' experience that transcended mere physical pleasure.

Images flashed behind his closed eyelids – memories that weren't his own, experiences he had never lived yet somehow felt with visceral immediacy. A moonlit forest from centuries past, trees towering in primeval majesty over a landscape untouched by modern development. A woman in elaborate dress, her throat exposed, fear and desire mingling in her expression as she offered herself to a younger Ritchie. The impressions came too quickly to grasp fully, dissolving into one another like dreams upon waking, leaving emotional residue without coherent narrative.

When Ritchie finally withdrew, reluctance

evident in the languid slowness of his movement, Tobias felt tears on his cheeks, though he couldn't have said what emotion had produced them. Joy, fear, wonder, loss – all seemed inadequate to explain the overwhelming experience of sharing Ritchie's consciousness, however briefly and incompletely.

"What happened?" he asked, his voice hoarse, sounding distant to his own ears. The room seemed to spin slightly around him, his perception altered by blood loss and the lingering effects of their connection. "I saw... things. Your memories?"

Ritchie looked genuinely surprised, an expression rarely seen on his normally composed features. He reached out to brush away the moisture on Tobias' cheeks, examining the tears on his fingertips with something like wonder. "You experienced my thoughts?"

Tobias nodded weakly, the movement requiring more effort than it should have, his body temporarily depleted by the feeding. "Fragments. Nothing clear. But I felt... I was there, in places I've never been, with people

I've never met." He struggled to articulate the disorientating experience of inhabiting memories not his own. "A forest. A woman."

Ritchie's expression shifted from surprise to something approaching awe, a rare vulnerability crossing his features as he processed this unprecedented development. "In all my years, through countless feedings..." He trailed off, seemingly at a loss for words – another rarity that underscored the significance of what had occurred. "I've heard of such connections in legend, whispered among my kind as myths. But I never believed..."

"Is it dangerous?" Tobias asked, though he found he didn't truly care about the answer. The experience of sharing Ritchie's consciousness, however briefly, had been profound beyond description – like discovering a new sense he hadn't known he lacked.

"Not dangerous," Ritchie said softly, his thumb tracing the curve of Tobias' cheekbone with reverent gentleness. "Extraordinary. Such psychic bonds are said to be incredibly rare." His voice held a note of wonder that Tobias had never heard before. "We are more deeply entwined than I ever anticipated."

Tobias reached up to touch the fresh puncture marks on his neck; they were already beginning to close. "I felt your satisfaction, your pleasure. But also…" He hesitated, struggling to articulate the complex emotions he'd experienced. "A kind of recognition. As though some part of you had been searching for something without knowing what it was, and found it in me."

Ritchie's eyes widened slightly – confirmation that Tobias had perceived correctly. "Yes," he admitted quietly. "That's precisely what I felt." He leaned forward, pressing his forehead gently against Tobias'. "You've unsettled centuries of careful control, Tobias Marlow. Made me feel things I had convinced myself were buried beyond resurrection."

They remained like that for a long moment, breathing together in the fire-lit darkness, both processing the magnitude of what had been revealed. The silence between them was comfortable rather than strained, filled with a new understanding that required no words.

Finally, Ritchie pulled back, his expression softening into something almost paternal in its tenderness. "You need rest now," he said. "The feeding always depletes you, and tonight's was... particularly intense."

Tobias nodded weakly, unable to argue as exhaustion pulled at him with increasing insistence.

With a restraint that spoke of centuries of practiced control, Ritchie reached down and adjusted the covers around Tobias' shoulders, ensuring he would remain warm as the fire died.

As silently as shadow itself, Ritchie moved to the door. He paused at the threshold, casting one final glance back. Then, without a word, he stepped out into the corridor, pulling the door closed with deliberate care to avoid even the slightest sound that might disturb Tobias' rest.

As Tobias drifted towards sleep in Ritchie's bed – another recent development in their relationship that spoke of increasing intimacy – he felt a strange contentment despite the warnings he'd received. The room grew dimmer as the fire settled into glowing embers, shadows reclaiming the corners in a comforting embrace. The prospect of transformation, of becoming something other than fully human, should have horrified him. Instead, it felt like fulfilment of a destiny he hadn't known was his until Ritchie entered his life.

His last conscious thought before surrendering to exhaustion was a mental image of himself transformed – stronger, eternal, forever bound to Ritchie by ties of blood and choice.

Chapter Six

Winter's grip on Ruehaven had loosened at last. The February evening held the first whispers of spring's eventual return, though frost still painted the windows of Caldwell Castle in delicate crystalline patterns. Ritchie stood at his study window, watching the sun's final descent behind the distant hills, calculating the precise moment when shadow would claim enough of the world to make venturing out safe. Behind him, he could hear Tobias moving about the room, organising papers with the meticulous care that had become second nature.

The months had transformed them both in ways Ritchie hadn't anticipated, even with centuries of experience to draw upon.

Love. The word had emerged between them gradually, first implied in gestures and glances, then whispered in moments of vulnerability, finally spoken with the conviction of certainty. Ritchie had believed himself beyond such mortal concerns, had thought his heart calcified by time into something incapable of that particular alchemy. Yet Tobias had proven him wrong with devastating thoroughness.

The memory of that pivotal night remained vivid in Ritchie's mind, replaying with the clarity that only vampiric recall could provide. He had instructed Tobias to kneel in the drawing room, hands clasped behind his head, wearing nothing but thin cotton undergarments that offered no protection against the castle's perpetual chill. A stress position designed to test endurance, to push Tobias towards that particular edge where discomfort transformed into something transcendent.

Ritchie had watched from his chair by the fire, ostensibly reading but in truth studying every minute shift in Tobias' posture, every tremor that ran through his increasingly strained muscles. Twenty minutes. Thirty. Forty-five. At the hour mark, tears had begun to track down Tobias' face, silent at first, then accompanied by soft, broken sobs that might have seemed like surrender to anyone who didn't know him as intimately as Ritchie did.

When Ritchie had finally given him permission to move, expecting the usual grateful collapse followed by the euphoric relief that typically accompanied release from such positions, Tobias had instead crawled forward on trembling limbs. Not to stretch, not to seek comfort, but to press desperate kisses to Ritchie's boots, words tumbling out between sobs that had nothing to do with physical discomfort.

"Please," Tobias had begged, his voice raw with emotion rather than strain. "I need to love you forever. I can't bear the thought of growing old while you remain unchanged. Of dying and leaving you alone again." More kisses, fevered and reverent. "Turn me. Make me yours completely. Let me exist by your side for eternity."

The memory still sent an unexpected flutter through Ritchie's chest – a sensation he'd thought lost to time. The depth of Tobias' yearning, the complete surrender not just of body but of mortality itself, had shaken something fundamental in Ritchie's carefully ordered existence.

"Ready?" Tobias asked now, pulling Ritchie from his reverie. The young man stood near the door, dressed impeccably in the dark wool coat Ritchie had commissioned for him, a deep burgundy scarf wound around his neck – partially for warmth, partially to conceal the fading marks from feeding.

"Almost," Ritchie replied, moving from the window. He approached Tobias, adjusting the scarf with careful fingers, using the gesture to study the face that had become so precious to him. The months of good food and care had restored Tobias fully – his cheeks held a healthy colour, and his eyes were bright with vitality that made the thought of extinguishing that mortal flame both thrilling and troubling.

They took the smaller coach, the one without the Caldwell crest, approaching Ruehaven from the eastern road that wound through the quieter residential district. As the horses' hooves clattered on the cobblestones, Ritchie found himself uncharacteristically nervous about the evening ahead. He had orchestrated this outing with deliberate intent, a test disguised as a simple excursion.

"The town seems livelier than usual," Tobias observed, peering out the window at the increasing foot traffic as they neared the centre.

"The winter market extends late on Fridays now," Ritchie explained, though he had known this when planning their visit. "The merchants guild petitioned for extended hours during the cold months."

As they disembarked near the old chapel – abandoned for decades and therefore perfectly discreet – Ritchie placed a hand on Tobias' arm, stilling him before they proceeded.

"I want you to observe everything tonight," he said, his voice carrying more than the simple instruction might suggest. "Really look at the world around you. Listen to it. Breathe it in." He met Tobias' questioning gaze directly. "Ask yourself, with complete honesty, if you're prepared to leave it all behind. Forever."

Understanding dawned in Tobias' eyes – this was not merely an evening outing but something far more significant. He nodded slowly, and Ritchie could see him beginning to approach their surroundings with new attentiveness.

They walked through the quieter streets first, past homes where families gathered for evening meals, windows glowing warm against the darkness. The domestic scenes were visible through gaps in curtains – a mother helping a child with needlework, a father reading aloud while his family listened, an elderly couple sharing tea in companionable silence.

Tobias watched it all, his expression thoughtful but unreadable. Ritchie found himself studying Tobias more than their surroundings, searching for signs of longing or regret, for any indication that the mortal world still held chains strong enough to bind him.

The market square, when they reached it, assaulted the senses with its vitality. Despite the cold, vendors had set up braziers that filled the air with smoke and warmth. The scent of roasting chestnuts mingled with fresh bread, spiced wine, and grilled meats. A group of musicians had established themselves near the fountain, their lively fiddle music drawing couples to dance despite the chill.

Children darted between the stalls, their laughter bright as they wove dangerously close to displays of winter vegetables and preserved goods. Young lovers walked arm in arm, sharing whispered conversations and stolen kisses when they thought no one was watching. Old men gathered around a chess table, arguing good-naturedly about a move while passing a flask between them.

It was humanity in all its chaotic, beautiful, temporary glory.

Ritchie watched Tobias take it all in – the way his nostrils flared at the cooking smells, how his foot tapped unconsciously to the music, the small smile that crossed his face when a child's wayward ball rolled to his feet and he returned it with gentle kindness.

"Shall we get something?" Tobias asked, gesturing towards a stall selling hot cider.

"If you'd like," Ritchie replied, though they both knew he wouldn't partake.

They acquired a cup of cider for Tobias, who wrapped his hands around it gratefully, inhaling the steam that rose from its surface. As he sipped, Ritchie noticed how Tobias' eyes tracked a young couple nearby – roughly his own age, the man whispering something that made the woman laugh and swat his arm playfully.

"They're newly married," Tobias observed quietly. "You can tell by how they keep touching each other, as if reassuring themselves the other is really there."

"You could have that," Ritchie said carefully. "A normal life. Marriage, children, growing old with someone who shares your mortality."

Tobias turned to look at him fully, and Ritchie was struck by the certainty in his expression. "I could," he agreed simply. "But that's not what I want."

They continued through the market, Ritchie deliberately guiding them past displays of life's simple pleasures – fresh flowers that would never again hold meaning for one who couldn't see them in sunlight, foods that would become ash in an immortal mouth, perfumes designed to mask the human scent that would become either torment or temptation.

A puppet show had drawn a crowd of children, their faces rapt as wooden figures acted out some moral tale. One small girl, perhaps five years old, stood at the edge of the group, craning her neck to see. Tobias crouched down beside her and quietly pointed out a gap between two older boys. "There's a better view there," he said kindly, waiting until she scampered forward, her face lighting up with delight. A nearby woman, presumably her mother, offered Tobias a grateful smile.

Ritchie felt something twist in his chest at the sight – Tobias would never have children of his own if turned. Never watch them grow, never pass on his gentle nature to a new generation. The enormity of what Tobias proposed to sacrifice pressed upon Ritchie with unexpected force.

When the puppet show ended and the child

returned to her mother with thank-yous all around, Tobias rejoined Ritchie with that same serene expression.

"You're good with children," Ritchie observed.

"I suppose I am," Tobias replied. "I hadn't really thought about it before."

"You should think about it now."

They left the market as the vendors began packing up their wares, the crowds thinning as families returned home for the night. The walk back to where their coach waited was quieter, both men lost in contemplation.

It was only when they were safely enclosed in the coach, returning to the castle, that Tobias spoke again.

"You think I haven't considered what I'd be giving up." It wasn't a question.

"I think you're young," Ritchie replied honestly. "I think you're in love, and that love makes any sacrifice seem worthwhile. But I've lived long enough to know that love, while powerful, doesn't erase the hardship of what's lost."

"And yet you loved before," Tobias pointed out. "Enough to turn someone."

Ritchie was quiet for a long moment, staring into nothing as he remembered. "I did. I turned her, as she asked. She seemed to accept it, even embrace it, but I still bear the weight of that choice. Sometimes I wonder if I did the right thing."

"I'm not her."

"No," Ritchie agreed. "You're not."

The remainder of the journey passed in contemplative silence.

Once back at the castle, Ritchie led Tobias to his private chambers – the same room where their blood bond had first revealed its unusual depth. The fire had been built up in their absence, casting warm light across the minimal furnishings.

"Kneel for me," Ritchie instructed, his voice gentle but carrying the authority that never failed to send a shiver through Tobias.

Tobias sank gracefully to his knees on the

thick carpet, assuming the position that had become second nature – back straight, hands resting palms-up on his thighs, eyes downcast but attentive. There was no stress in this position, no challenge. Ritchie simply wanted to look at him, to study this remarkable creature who had wandered into his life and transformed it so thoroughly.

Ritchie circled slowly, taking in every detail. The way the firelight caught the gold in Tobias' hair, making it gleam like spun silk. The steady rise and fall of his chest, breathing regulated as Ritchie had taught him. The complete stillness that spoke of absolute trust, of surrender so complete it had become its own form of strength.

This beautiful, fragile, temporary being had given himself entirely to Ritchie's keeping. Not just his body, not just his obedience, but his very soul, offered up with a generosity that still humbled Ritchie tremendously.

Ritchie remembered finding Tobias in that stable, surrounded by brutes who understood nothing of the treasure they were mishandling. Even then, debased and abused, there had been something luminous about him. Not innocence – Tobias had never been innocent in the conventional sense – but rather a quality of recognition, as if their souls had known each other across time and had finally found their way back together.

Since that fateful day, that recognition had deepened into something Ritchie had no adequate words for. Love seemed too simple, too mortal a term for what existed between them. It was recognition and possession, dominance and devotion, need and fulfilment all twisted together into something that defied easy categorisation.

Tobias had submitted to him in ways that went far beyond the physical. He had opened his mind through their bond, sharing thoughts and memories with an intimacy most vampires never achieved with their chosen companions. He had embraced not just Ritchie's darkness but his own, finding liberation in desires that society would condemn.

And now he knelt here, patient and perfect, awaiting Ritchie's decision about their eternal future together.

Ritchie reached out, fingers carding gently through Tobias' hair, feeling the young man lean subtly into the touch while maintaining his position. Such discipline, learnt so quickly and employed so beautifully. Tobias embraced submission as if born for it, finding in service a fulfilment that transcended mere obedience.

"Look at me," Ritchie commanded softly.

Tobias raised his eyes, and Ritchie was struck anew by their clarity. No fear, no uncertainty, just that steady blue gaze that seemed to see through all of Ritchie's centuries of carefully constructed walls.

They stayed like that for a long moment, vampire and mortal, predator and willing prey, dominant and submissive, two halves of something that finally felt whole.

Ritchie thought of the market, of all the mortal pleasures Tobias had witnessed without a flicker of regret or longing. He thought of how good Tobias had been with the children, the future generations that would never come to be. He thought of sunrises Tobias would never see again, of foods that would turn to ash in his mouth, of the terrible hunger that would replace all other appetites.

He thought, too, of centuries stretching ahead without Tobias. Of watching him age, watching vitality fade from those clear eyes, watching death claim him as it claimed all mortals. The thought was unexpectedly unbearable, a pain sharp enough to pierce.

But the decision could not be his alone, no matter how much he might wish to simply claim Tobias permanently. The transformation required more than just blood – it required a willingness, a complete surrender to the change. Tobias would need to choose it not just with his heart but with full understanding of the consequences.

"Rise," Ritchie instructed finally.

Tobias stood smoothly, awaiting further direction.

"You've seen the world tonight," Ritchie said. "Felt its warmth, tasted its pleasures, witnessed its simple joys. I want you to think about what you experienced. Really consider it, not through the lens of our love but as its own truth."

"For how long?" Tobias asked.

"As long as you need. Days, weeks, months if necessary." Ritchie cupped Tobias' face in his hands, thumbs stroking over cheekbones with infinite tenderness. "This decision, once made, cannot be unmade. I need to know – we both need to know – that it's made with complete understanding."

Tobias nodded, leaning into Ritchie's touch. "I understand."

"Do you? Do you truly comprehend that the mortal world will become forever closed to you? That you'll watch people you might care about age and die? That the hunger will be with you always, demanding satisfaction?"

"I understand," Tobias repeated, steadier this time. "But I also understand what I gain. Eternity with you. The chance to love you not just for a mortal lifetime but forever. The opportunity to serve you, to belong to you, completely and permanently."

The words sent a possessive thrill through Ritchie that he didn't try to suppress. The thought of Tobias as his eternal companion, forever his, was intoxicating.

But he had been here before, had felt this certainty with another who later came to different conclusions. He would not make the same mistake twice.

"Think carefully about it," Ritchie said, releasing Tobias' face reluctantly. "And when you're certain – absolutely certain – tell me."

Tobias smiled, an expression of such serene confidence that it made Ritchie's chest tighten. "I will," he promised. "Though I suspect my answer won't change."

As Ritchie drew Tobias into his arms, feeling the mortal warmth of him, the steady heartbeat that marked his humanity, he found himself hoping that was true. The prospect of eternity stretched before him, as it always had, but for the first time in centuries, it didn't seem like a burden to carry but a gift to share.

With Tobias.

Forever, if the young man chose it.

And deep in his soul, Ritchie found himself praying to forces he no longer believed in that Tobias would.

Epilogue

And so it was that spring had fully claimed Ruehaven before Ritchie and Tobias embarked upon the ultimate journey together. The weeks following their visit into the town that night had been ones of careful contemplation, of watching and waiting, of ensuring that the magnitude of their decision was met with equal certainty. Tobias had taken Ritchie's counsel to heart, spending long nights in quiet reflection, examining his choice from every angle as the last snows melted and the first green shoots pushed through the thawing earth. Ritchie, for his part, had given him space while remaining watchful, searching for any sign of doubt or regret that might suggest hesitation. Only when the spring equinox had passed, when both were absolutely certain that this path was chosen with full understanding of its irreversible nature, did they begin.

They both knew the transformation would not be swift, but rather a gradual metamorphosis requiring multiple exchanges of blood over weeks, each feeding carefully orchestrated with deliberate intent to reshape Tobias' mortal essence into something eternal.

The first feeding with transformative purpose took place in the castle's oldest chamber, a vaulted room that had witnessed centuries pass in silent observation. Ritchie had prepared it with meticulous care: hundreds of candles casting dancing shadows across stone walls, white silk sheets that seemed to glow in the golden light, and roses – deep crimson roses whose petals had been scattered across every surface, their scent heavy in the air like a benediction. When Ritchie's fangs pierced Tobias' throat that night, it was not merely to feed but to begin the sacred process of remaking.

The pleasure that crashed through Tobias' body at that first transformative bite was beyond anything their previous exchanges had offered – a rapture so intense it drew cries from his lips that echoed off the ancient stones, his body arching beneath Ritchie's as waves of ecstasy merged with the profound intimacy of their bonding, each pull at his throat sending pulses of sensation that left him trembling and gasping, suspended in a state of blissful surrender that seemed to stretch into eternity itself. For Ritchie, the experience was equally transcendent – the taste of Tobias' willing blood carried not just sustenance but the intoxicating essence of complete submission, the power flooding through him with a potency that made his centuries-old control falter, his own deep moans vibrating against Tobias' throat as he drank, feeling the exquisite rush of dominance made manifest in this most intimate act of possession, claiming not just blood but the very soul of the one who offered himself so completely.

Over time, the changes came gradually, as Ritchie had foretold. First, Tobias noticed his senses sharpening – colours became more vivid even as sunlight grew painful, sounds previously inaudible now rang clear as bells, and scents told stories his mortal nose had never perceived. His body grew stronger, as though gravity's hold had loosened its jealous grip. The hunger began as a whisper, then grew to a roar that sometimes frightened him with its intensity. There were nights when Tobias wept at the strangeness of his changing form, mourning the simple humanity that slipped away with each exchange of blood. His reflection grew paler, his eyes began to hold depths that hadn't existed before, and food turned to ash on his tongue while a different appetite awakened within.

Yet true to his nature, Tobias approached even this ultimate transformation with the same devoted submission he had brought to every other challenge Ritchie had set before him. When the hunger clawed at his throat, he knelt at Ritchie's feet and accepted instruction in control. When his changing body rebelled against its metamorphosis, he endured with the patience of one who understood that all worthwhile surrenders require sacrifice. His love for Ritchie became the anchor that held him steady through the storm of transformation, his submission not weakness but the greatest strength – the conscious choice to trust another with his very essence, to allow himself to be remade in the image of their shared desire.

Early summer had arrived by the time the

transformation was complete, though neither of them would see it in daylight again. They stood together at the castle window in those precious minutes before dawn, two figures whose eternal bond had been sealed in blood and choice. Where once there had been master and servant, dominant and submissive, vampire and mortal, now there existed something far more profound – two halves of a single whole, bound by threads stronger than death itself.

In Tobias, Ritchie had found not merely a companion for eternity but the one soul in all his centuries who could meet his darkness with equal shadow, who could surrender so completely that dominance became an act of worship rather than mere control. In Ritchie, Tobias had discovered the firm hand he had always craved, the strength that could contain his submission without breaking it, the ancient wisdom that could guide him through pleasures and pains he had never dared imagine. Together, they had created something that transcended the simple categories of love or lust, dominance or submission – they had forged a connection that would endure long after the castle itself crumbled to dust, after the last mortals who remembered them had passed into legend.

The centuries that stretched before them no longer seemed like a curse but a privilege to be savoured, each year another opportunity to explore the infinite variations of their desire, to push boundaries that would never break because they were built on absolute trust. They had found in each other the missing pieces of their souls, the parts that spoke to needs both carnal and romantic, creating a love that was at once tender and terrible, gentle and consuming, eternal as the darkness they now shared. And in that darkness, paradoxically, they had found the greatest light of all – the illumination that comes from being perfectly seen, perfectly known, and perfectly possessed by another for all time.